"I don't acc supremacy," she deem

His golden eyes mocked her. "You know what your problem is, Sara? You're so angry at men you can't really love them. You need help." He caught hold of her and arched her back over his arm, his mouth dangerously close to her own.

"Let me go, Guy," she gasped, aware she was almost panting through her half-open lips.

"Easy, little filly." He laughed gently and pulled her closer. "Is it possible that you're experiencing something you don't want to?"

"All right, then. Kiss me!" she dared him furiously.

Sara felt a terrible kind of inevitability when the absolute mastery of his kiss swept aside everything else. . . .

Margaret Way takes great pleasure in her work and works hard at her pleasure. She enjoys tearing off to the beach with her family on weekends, loves haunting galleries and auctions and is completely given over to French champagne "for every possible joyous occasion." Her home, perched high on a hill overlooking Brisbane, Australia, is her haven. She started writing when her son was a baby, and now she finds there is no better way to spend her time.

Books by Margaret Way

HARLEQUIN ROMANCE

2609—HOUSE OF MEMORIES
2634—ALMOST A STRANGER
2639—NO ALTERNATIVE
2658—A PLACE CALLED RAMBULARA
2700—FALLEN IDOL
2724—EAGLE'S RIDGE
2784—THE TIGER'S CAGE
2820—INNOCENT IN EDEN
2832—DIAMOND VALLEY
2939—MORNING GLORY

Don't miss any of our special offers. Write to us at the following address for information on our newest releases.

Harlequin Reader Service
901 Fuhrmann Blvd., P.O. Box 1397, Buffalo, NY 14240
Canadian address: P.O. Box 603,
Fort Erie, Ont. L2A 5X3

Devil Moon

Margaret Way

Harlequin Books

TORONTO • NEW YORK • LONDON
AMSTERDAM • PARIS • SYDNEY • HAMBURG
STOCKHOLM • ATHENS • TOKYO • MILAN

Original hardcover edition published in 1988
by Mills & Boon Limited

ISBN 0-373-02958-6

Harlequin Romance first edition January 1989

CHAPTER ONE

THEY followed a gold Mercedes almost all the way to the airport, a superb 500 SEC, and as Sara stood out on the pavement rummaging for the taxi fare, she glanced with mild curiosity at the two men who alighted from it. One was silver-haired, sixtyish, canny-eyed, conservatively dressed: a Cabinet Minister. The other...well, the other was the kind of man who made Sara's mind jangle. Such men aroused sharp memories of her father: immutably *male*. The kind of men who made women feel powerless. The kind who accepted male domination as the natural order. Instinctively she hardened her heart to them, in essence a defence mechanism and very deeply entrenched.

Yet she was struck by his face. It went way beyond handsome, being bold and aggressive. It was the sort of face to cause discomfort. It was the timeless face of a conqueror. Flaring nostrils over a fine, curling mouth. Cleft chin, sloped Slavic cheekbones. His dark golden skin was stretched to extreme tautness over these absurdly dominant features. Even his hair was remarkable: jet-black shot with copper. It curled crisply to his scalp and broad forehead and was worn rather full and long.

He was very tall. Six-three, maybe six-four in those fancy boots. Wide-shouldered, lean, loose and rangy. By contrast to his companion he was dressed casually: deep-pocketed beige bush shirt with silver-buttoned epaulettes, close-fitting stretch jeans, rust-coloured belt with an elaborate silver clasp around his supple waist.

A primitive, she thought. Someone powerful, elemental for all the polished veneer. She had never seen such a physical flaunting of male beauty and power. Her heart turned icy and she began to look away, but as she did so he swung abruptly like a creature bred to strike swiftly and pierced her with his eyes.

They were _gold_. An incredible gleaming topaz like a jungle cat's. They locked with hers so that the swirling movement and noise of the crowd queerly faded. Her frozen heart fluttered, then gave a hard pang of panic. It was instinct reminding her of all the hard lessons she had learned in life.

'Thatsa six dollars thirty, love.' The taxi-driver's pronounced Italian accent came at her. 'Six dollar to you.'

Sara blinked her swimming eyes. 'It was five dollars thirty on the meter.'

'Dollar for the call, love.'

'Oh, I'm sorry.' She gave him a sudden, apologetic smile and his admiring glance turned almost to adoration. A repetition of countless looks Sara had received since she had made the transition from child to young woman.

'Haven't I seen you on the telly?'

'You could have.' She put the fare into his hand. 'I'm a journalist on the Evan Kirkman show.' _Was_ a journalist, she thought between anger and pain.

'You're beautiful!' he told her loudly.

'Thank you.' She gave him a faintly brittle smile. 'I'm a good journalist too.' Sara had never in her life overvalued a woman's physical charms, least of all her own. What _she_ was about was accomplishments.

'Thatsa quite a lot!' He stood back saluting her. 'But a beautiful woman is God's greatest creation. She doesn't need to be anything else.'

Sara didn't even attempt to argue. Men were valued for their intelligence. Women were valued for their beauty, sexuality, whatever. Man was handed every means to fulfil himself. Woman had to fight for it. Her father, an eminent QC, had bitterly opposed her desire to read law, and to give her mother an easier time she had surrendered and settled for an arts degree, majoring in journalism. Women were silly, irrational, sentimental. They had no objectivity. No mental or emotional control. Dear God! Her father was a highly respected man. A man with a public and private identity.

Sara shook herself free of her dismal thoughts. It had been a traumatic time of late. She wondered what a psychiatrist would make of her aversion to dominant authority figures. Drat that man with the golden eyes.

Streams of people were arriving now, and Sara looked around quickly for a trolley. She only had two pieces of luggage but they were fairly heavy. A party of students blocked her way, but as she made her way around them, a woman with tears streaming down her face made a mad dash for the only visible empty trolley and grabbed it, the tears not unmixed now with a sudden, fierce triumph.

'Damn!' Sara swore beneath her breath. Maybe they were tears of joy?

'Please, have mine.'

She knew before she turned who spoke to her. She had even sensed his presence, like one wild animal might another. His voice was a dark, deep, confident purr.

'Is that an order?' She swung about, colour in her flawless white skin, eyes very green against her glowing hair. She could feel the familiar rising anger, illogical but powerful.

'If you take orders.' He was looking at her with extraordinary attention. Probably thinking she was mad.

'Independence is more my line.'

'Really?' He gave her a faintly humouring, satiric smile. 'I thought you the sort of woman who always had men dancing attendance.' He stowed her luggage with careless strength, then turned it towards her. 'I won't presume to push it for you.'

'Thank you.' The words came out as though they choked her.

'No bother at all.' He gave her another of his distinctive, piercing glances.

That was Encounter One.

Ten minutes later Sara was seated in the lounge waiting for the call to board the aircraft. She had spotted the tall, dark man several seats away and deliberately turned her back, a piece of studied rudeness he strangely seemed to enjoy.

What was the matter with her, for God's sake? She only had to see a man who reminded her of her father and her nerves were in a rage. There was no question that the traumas of childhood and adolescence, though they could be surmounted, left indelible scars.

The 737 they would be flying on was being refuelled. She never sat in an airport anywhere without being uncomfortably aware of the frailty of life. She had flown all over the world, the daughter of a rich man. She should have been the most blessed of creatures; instead she was only determined. It hadn't been easy challenging a man for her rights. That was the difference between her and her mother, and she loved her mother dearly.

A hand grasped her shoulder and Sara looked around in surprise.

'Evan!' A sick anger exploded inside her.

'I had to see you.' He dropped into the seat beside her. 'Don't get mad. Whatever problem you're having, I'll solve it.' He took her hand in his.

'How would you start?'

'Keep your voice down, Sara. You wouldn't have to be a detective to recognise me.' Evan Kirkman's boyish, blond good looks were as familiar to most television viewers as their own, though he was short, slighter than he appeared on the small screen.

'So why come here, Evan?' Sara muttered fiercely. 'This is harassment.'

'Oh, for God's sake, leave off that feminist stuff.'

'Then what would you call it?' she challenged him. 'Has it occurred to you because of your attentions I'm out of a job?'

'You're not out of a job, you quit.'

'Hey now.' She pulled her hand back with all her strength. 'We could finish up on national TV.'

'Then you'd *have* to take me seriously.'

'I'm happy the way I am!' Sara stalked to the window but he followed her, a moth to the flame.

'How can you do this to Liz?' She twisted a bracelet around her arm. 'Can't you settle for a wife and family?'

'With girls like you around?' He laughed grimly. 'I never want to stop looking at you. Liz is OK. We have an open marriage.'

'The hell you do!' she told him scornfully. 'Liz doesn't play around. She's developed as a human being. She's committed to her *husband*.'

'She loves me. It's different for men. They feel sexy all the time. Wanting a woman is just like breathing.'

'Well, don't hold your breath for me!' Sara shook back her red-gold mane. 'Obviously it comes hard but I'm totally against polygamy.'

'I require more out of life, Sara,' Evan told her by way of excuse. 'Anyway, most women don't have a fine, free nature like you. They revel in being subordinate to their men!'

'Oh, drop dead!' Sara felt so violently she almost shouted back. 'What *you* can't accept is, there are masses and masses of women who see themselves as individuals and this individual isn't even vaguely attracted to you. I know it's an awful revelation but there it is. I'm going to another man this minute.'

'You mean you're running away.'

'You bet I am. I'm thoroughly cheesed off. You made real use of your position to try and pressurise me into a sexual relationship.'

'I did nothing of the kind!'

There was a dangerous gleam in Sara's green eyes. 'You know I'm ambitious, so using my ambition was part of the plan. The only hitch was that I'm fed up with your atrocious infantile ego, and what's more, all your erotic fantasies are stuck in adolescence. The ones I'm sorry for are Liz and your kids. They deserve more.'

'I'll divorce her.' Evan's understanding of her argument was not based on reason but male psychology. He actually thought she was hanging out for a declaration.

'Boy, what a solution!' Sara was so enraged she could have gnashed her teeth. 'I don't *want* you, Evan, and I have never in word or action given you the slightest encouragement beyond showing I enjoyed working on the show.'

'You could go to the top, Sara. If I let you.'

'No thanks!' Her eyes flared at him. 'If I can't get to the top without sacrificing my principles, I'll just have to change direction. I'm bright. I'll make out.'

'You need me. Every bit as much as I need you. We're a team. Maybe I've made too strong a play, but you act so damned self-assured I didn't realise you're just a girl. I'm not thinking too clearly myself, but I do know one thing: you make me so excited, I'm dizzy. I could forget right now we're in a public place.'

She nearly jumped. 'You'd better not!'

Her glittering eyes were indescribable, like emeralds. 'You've got problems, Sara,' he assured her. 'One of them is your temper.'

'Sure is.' It was the only true word he had spoken. 'Please leave me alone, Evan.'

'I won't, *can't*. Not until you promise to come back to the show.'

'This is hell, really hell!' Sara was uncomfortably aware lots of people were staring. 'The answer is *no*, Evan.'

'Bitch!' He grasped her cruelly in his despair, staring down into her vivid face. Conniver that he was, he was about to lose his head—only a dark, commanding voice boomed in his ear.

'I'd cut the goodbyes if I were you. It's time to go!'

'Wh-what?' Evan spun around, first with hostility, then dumb shock. 'Who the hell are you?'

'Sara's ... friend,' the masterful man said simply.

Clearly he was telling her to play along and Sara rushed to him warmly and clung on to his arm. 'Darling, you do know Evan Kirkman?' Her eyes filled with a phoney, utterly convincing soft ardency.

'I know your show, of course, Kirkman.' The big man extended his hand, subjecting Evan to a painful grip. 'Never find time to watch it.'

'Pity, most people do.' Evan's fair skin wore a dark flush. 'I never realised Sara was ... involved.'

'Well, she is.' The tall man looked indulgent, possessive and dangerous. 'Trenton's the name. Guy Trenton.'

'Really?' Evan looked confounded, hesitating because the name rang a bell.

'Trenton Estates.' Sara had it in less than a minute. 'You mean you're the one-time engineer with the big tea plantation up north?'

'I certainly am.'

'That's right, Evan,' Sara cooed. 'You'll have to hear the rest of it another time.'

'Sara!' Evan, the inveterate philanderer, looked shocked.

'Go home to your wife, Kirkman,' the big man warned quietly. 'Take my advice. All women are mysteries, but *this* one didn't mean a word of what she told you.'

'Told him!' Sara exploded.

'Quiet. It's all right,' Guy Trenton told her in a very dominant tone.

'Sara, we've got to talk about this.' Evan almost skipped alongside them as the tall, powerful Trenton urged Sara along.

'Try to be brave!' Trenton turned abruptly and all but pinned Evan to the plate-glass window.

'Now look here, Trenton,' Evan wavered.

'No, you look here.' It was a subdued growl. 'I could fix it that you wouldn't be able to show your pretty face for weeks but that would be uncivilised and messy. Accept what Sara was trying to tell you. She doesn't love you, love you any more, whatever.'

'And she's going off with you?'

'What did she tell you?'

'She said she was going to some guy.'

'Well then.' The tall man put his arm very casually around Sara's slim shoulders. 'You know what they say, all's fair in love and war.' He sounded both amused and contemptuous.

'I suppose I should thank you,' Sara gritted after Evan, flushed and humiliated, raced away.

'Fooling around with another woman's man can't make you feel good about yourself?'

'Don't try judging me!' Sara's green eyes flashed up. 'I quit my job.'

'And a new man already?' He looked at her as if she had an ungovernable urge to add scalps to her belt.

Take it easy…easy…she calmed herself. Probably she would never see him again.

'What's his name?'

'Mind your own business,' she said icily.

'Ingratitude, thou marble-hearted fiend!'

'I *did* say thank you.'

'You said——' he showed his boarding pass to the attendant and picked up the conversation when they were outside the door '—I *suppose* I should thank you. What you meant was: I wish to God it had been anyone but *you*!'

'Oh?' She flashed him a grudging look of respect 'Mind-reader, are you?'

'Seldom have I seen a more transparent face. In fact your expressions are so great you should be in movies.'

Wryly she shook her head. 'I suppose if you knew, so would others?'

'Certainly the ones looking your way. At one stage we all thought you were going to give way to the reckless urge to smack his face.'

'I do remember my hand tingling.'

Nonchalantly he took her heavy shoulder-bag from her, his mocking smile defying her to object. 'Something about me bother you?'

'If I saw your photograph in the paper I'd expect the caption: Hero Returns Home; or: Guy Trenton Photographed Beside his Lear Jet.'

'I do fly a plane if you must know. Not a Lear jet. I would have thought heroes would be viewed with admiration.'

'Of course. Men are bred to high adventure. We all fall down in idolatry of the glorious male.'

He glanced down at her and laughed, his burnished eyes sweeping over her beautiful, long-limbed body and high-bred face. 'My God, aren't *women* the worshipped of the species? Don't tell me you don't use *your* beauty to crack the whip? I guess Kirkman has a really nice wife at home but I'll bet she doesn't come into the "man-trap" category like you.'

'Monster!' Sara's blood turned molten. She reached out and grabbed her bag back. 'You don't understand anything at all.'

'Oh, I understand well enough,' he jeered softly.

That was Encounter Two.

They were separated by virtue of the seating, and for that Sara was immensely grateful. Men like that pulled her in different directions. Deep down they terrified her because she was attracted to them as well. It was one of the complexities of her woman's nature. Obviously he thought she had been having an affair with Evan and decided to call it off. What did she care what he thought anyway? Many quick solutions were achieved through a man's physical strength. Certainly Evan hadn't wanted to tackle such a superb specimen.

For the past year Sara had been working on and off on a first novel: a doomed love story based on life. In fact it was largely based on her parents' extraordinary marriage. Her father had a brilliant legal mind, yet that same mind absolutely denied corresponding brilliance in a woman. They could aspire, they could never *be*. In general they were only clever at domestic life and a lot of the time not even then. Her mother had come to her marriage at the tender age of nineteen, beautiful, sensitive, cultured. She had been deeply in love with her brilliant young husband, though he was ten years older and already beginning to devastate her with his intellectual assertiveness. Their relationship had been based on sexual passion and the fact that Paula Bernard came from a highly respected family. Outwardly all through the marriage they presented a marvellously complementary image, only Sara and one or two others became aware of Miles Richardson's underlying cruelty. In public he was the acid-tongued, suave charmer. In private, a harsh and overbearing despot.

Why hadn't her mother left him? Because *she* trapped her. Her mother's greatest fear had always been that somehow she would be robbed of her daughter. Her husband had no scruples. He was absolutely ruthless and he had a vast knowledge of the law and how to make it work for him. Sara had suffered as a child and even more as a rebellious adolescent. Writing about it was a therapy. She had none of her mother's constraint, although she had inherited her mother's beauty and exquisite colouring. She was outgoing and fiery, more like the grandmother she had lost, fighting her father with what she didn't realise was great bravery. Her father was a natural oppressor, rigidly unsympathetic to women though he attracted them in droves. This Sara saw as a double cruelty to her mother. At one stage, during her first year at university, she had consulted a psychiatrist in a vain attempt to help her sort out the unhappy complexities of her family life. She wanted desperately to leave home but couldn't bear to leave her mother, and he had obviously thought she was fantasising. Her father's public image was too secure. After that, she kept it all to herself, schooling herself to blandness with her father and offering her mother all the compassion and support she could muster. It said a great deal for her character that she impressed people as a bright and confident girl. In public her father maintained a façade of great pride in his womenfolk. In private he lived to confuse and belittle them. Sara always described him to her mother as a schizophrenic and her mother though incredibly loyal never actually denied it. All this Sara had been endeavouring to turn into a work of fiction. Sometimes she thought she was bringing it off, it was all so very real to her; other times she thought the outpourings of heart and mind could only be of interest to herself.

Now as she tried to plot another chapter in her mind her concentration was diminished by recurring

thoughts of Guy Trenton. His whole aura made her
heart flutter. Not with fascination but a kind of
nervous frenzy. No matter how long or how hard she
had trained herself, she had her mother's thin skin.
His interference, rescue, whatever, had astounded her.
His arbitrary assumption that she used her beauty-
sexuality as a weapon made her blood boil. It was
difficult to control her instinctive antipathy to the
man. She wondered wryly if he was married. Another
master/slave relationship? She felt certain he would
be superlative in bed. By such chains were women
bound.

Sara turned off her unwelcome thoughts and tried
to think about Wayne. She hadn't seen him for about
a month, but on the phone he had sounded more her
friend than ever. Wayne was a painter. Not one of
the artists' colony to seek the peace and tropical
splendour of North Queensland. Wayne had been
born in the sugar lands, country he still painted in
such vivid fashion, but nowadays he moved between
a Barrier Reef island retreat and his mother's re-
tirement property in the cooler climate of the ranges.
Now that she thought about it, they couldn't be far
from the Trenton Estates. She remembered reading
years ago how a Philip Trenton had announced his
plans to pioneer a great tea industry. So far as she
could recall, the Trenton family had come from
Ceylon. She had an idea the government of Sri Lanka
had taken over their vast estates and they had tried
to re-establish themselves in New Guinea before
seeking the stability of Australia. It was said the soil
of the north was so rich anything would grow. Philip
Trenton had created his own tea industry. She supposed Guy might be his son, though he had spent a
good many years building bridges. Wayne would
probably know him, or of him. They had to be some
six or seven years apart. She was twenty-three, Wayne
was twenty-seven and Guy Trenton had to be thirty-

three or four. There was a whole lot of living packed into that face.

She remembered how she had met Wayne Palmer. Evan had sent her to interview him after a sell-out showing. His gentle, whimsical manner, rather diffident and reserved when she had been expecting something more flamboyant, had intrigued her; his somewhat faun-like appearance, very slender, a golden-brown crown of curls and slanted brown eyes. He couldn't be persuaded to talk much about himself. He kept his more passionate feelings for his art, and then he was extremely articulate and able to pitch it at a level the average viewer would be able to understand and appreciate. It all made for excellent television, and they had kept up the friendship. It even seemed ordained that he rang on the very night Sara resigned under pressure, for as soon as he heard, he begged her to visit his world. There were so many places he could take her, and surely she needed the break. The very next morning his mother rang to extend a personal invitation. So it had been arranged. A few weeks in Paradise. Wasn't that what they called the tropical north?

It was a smooth, uneventful flight and Wayne met her on touch-down, quickly detaching her from the waiting crowd.

'Sara, how wonderful to have you here!' His kiss of greeting which began at her cheek somehow slipped to her mouth. 'You look a dream, as usual.' His slanted brown eyes were alive with excitement.

'How long is it before we catch the charter flight?' she asked him.

'If you turn around you can see it. Just four of us, I think. I'd say we'll take off as soon as the luggage is aboard.'

'I've never flown in a light aircraft before.' Sara, who was feeling her way just a little, turned to face him.

'Not nervous, are you?' He took her arm and rubbed it, slipping easily, instantly into another mode, more lover-like than friendly.

'I always like to know what I'm letting myself in for.' Sara said it lightly but her eyes locked with his. On no account was she going to be rushed, and she wanted him to know it.

He seemed to get the message, because he dropped his hand and gave her an uncomplicated smile. 'All right, let's get your luggage. It'll only take a moment. Wait right here.'

'Thank you, Wayne.' Sara smiled at him and walked to the window. Outside was a blazing blue and gold world, so much hotter than she expected she had slipped off the sand-coloured linen jacket that went with her slacks. The new arrivals were being met by people very casually and colourfully dressed in accordance with the character of the tropical north and the hordes of tourists that followed the sun. The country they had flown over looked magnificent; hundreds of square miles of canefields under an electric blue sky, and behind them the jungle-clad walls of the Dividing Range. Sara's mind reverted to aircraft again. So many times in recent history light aircraft had gone down in the jungle. In a continent of vast distances flying one's own aircraft was a way of life. She couldn't help recalling the jungles of the north were said to be so dense they were almost impossible to penetrate. It didn't make her all that eager to fly over them, though her nagging little anxieties, she realised, were probably brought on by the loss of her job. Sara pushed the heavy, deep waves of her hair, deciding she would pin it up as soon as she was able. It really was hot and she pondered the likelihood of an afternoon storm, though on this vivid September day it was months off the monsoon season.

Wayne brought back her luggage, giving her a frank, open smile. 'Are you sure you're not an apparition?'

'I'm real and I'm here for two weeks!'

They heard the call to board the charter flight and they began to walk. 'Val is so looking forward to meeting you,' Wayne told her. 'She worries about me, you know.'

'No, I didn't know.' Sara smiled at him.

'I think she feels I'm getting to be so much of a recluse I don't get to make many friends.'

'Didn't you tell me you were once engaged?'

'Yep!' He gave a wry laugh. 'It was pretty hasty altogether. It was over in three months.'

'How long did it hurt?'

'Not long. I've learnt to dissociate myself through my work.'

They were half-way to the twin-engined light plane before they spotted the couple walking slowly from the administrative block. The man was moving with a now familiar striking suppleness, the woman, young, tall, thin, very trendily attired, was looking up at him and laughing, her teeth, even at a distance, very white against her golden tanned skin.

Encounter Three.

Sara was so disconcerted she came to an abrupt halt and Wayne, just to top it, burst out in what sounded like a panic: 'My God, it's Trenton, and Leigh's with him.'

Their sudden halt and looking back had the effect of inducing Guy Trenton to raise a hand and so did the woman, but more slowly and less expansively.

'I take it you know them both?' Sara enquired.

'Everyone knows Trenton up here.' Wayne jerked a hand through his tousled curls. 'Leigh, believe it or not, is the girl I was engaged to.'

'And now you don't know what to do?' Sara asked, caught between humour and disbelief.

'I'll manage. These days we move in opposite circles.'

'We meet again,' Guy Trenton greeted Sara suavely.

'It's as they always say: it's a small world.'

'It is indeed.' He gave her a faintly mocking smile. 'How goes it, Wayne?'

'Great!' Wayne's answering smile was obviously forced. 'I hardly expected to see *you* on a charter flight, Guy. Or you either, Leigh.' Only now did he turn to acknowledge Guy Trenton's companion, who appeared as much taken by surprise as he was.

'But then you never did keep up with things, did you?' she challenged him, antagonism emanating from her thin frame. 'Guy doesn't take delivery of his new toy for another month.'

'Lucky Guy!'

'Lucky nothing!' Guy Trenton said in that voice that so easily commanded attention. 'Everything I've got I've worked damned hard for. And I won't tolerate my new plane being called a toy. It's a work-horse.'

'Darling, I'm sorry. That wasn't very tactful.' The dark girl grasped his arm and clung to it.

'You're forgiven.' He looked down and smiled at her but Sara thought she detected a faint coolness in those burning eyes.

'I gather you've met Sara, Guy?' Wayne asked of the older man.

'Just recently, at the airport.' Sara raised her green eyes to a gaze that locked them.

'Through a mutual friend,' Guy Trenton confirmed in his mocking voice.

'Really?' the dark girl asked abruptly, turning back to her careful head-to-toe assessment of Sara. 'Anyone we know?'

'Evan Kirkman,' Sara replied, merely to get it over.

'That's how Sara and I met,' Wayne explained almost ingratiatingly, his brown eyes on Sara's creamy face and glorious hair. 'I'm sorry, I haven't introduced you two girls. Sara Richardson, Leigh Sutton.'

'Nice to meet you,' Sara smiled, but didn't extend her hand sensing the other's sharp reserve.

'Not another artist, are you?'

'Nothing so wonderful. I'm a journalist.'

The dark girl laughed at the idea. 'I haven't much time for any of them,' she announced, attempting to soften her aggressive attitude with a show of amusement.

'No worries,' Sara said lightly. 'The great thing about a democracy is everyone can have an opinion, no matter how far removed from informed.'

'Shall we go on?' Guy Trenton asked suavely. 'I expect Jake is waiting to take off.'

He led the way, of course, greeting the pilot who appeared to know him well, chatting amiably on the tarmac while the others went aboard. He was a man who assumed a natural, easy authority, and though she had sensed a lack of cordiality between him and Wayne, the pilot had greeted him with pleasure and respect. Sara had seen it in the man's eyes.

The plane was a six-seater. Guy Trenton eventually settled up front near the cockpit so that he could talk to the pilot, Leigh Sutton went to join him and Sara and Wayne sat across the aisle from each other towards the rear.

'Of all the rotten luck!' Wayne whispered wryly. 'Guy and Leigh were the last people I expected to see. Guy always flies his own plane, and God knows what Leigh is doing here. Probably flaunting her new relationship.'

'Does it upset you?'

'Yes. Yes, it does a bit, but there's nothing I can do about it either. I want this trip of yours to be perfect. I want it to bring us closer together.'

'Instead, what's happened?' she asked with a quizzical smile.

'Trenton always rubs me up the wrong way,' Wayne admitted. 'He's one of those madly determined types who succeed at everything they do, and Leigh has always made me feel...inadequate. I'll never know why she ever consented to become engaged to me. Nearly everything I've ever done annoys her.'

'She's not proud of your work?'

Wayne's attractive face was filled with a hopeless anger. 'Any mention of my "work" brings out the worst in her. Leigh's people have always been land-owners. Too big to be called farmers. All of them belong to a group that think it inappropriate for a man to draw for a living. To them it's a way of life that's unstable and fraught with uncertainty. I suppose it is. Again, what would the history of civilisation have been without its artists?'

'I shudder to think!' Sara cast a thoughtful glance towards Leigh's glossy head. 'Yet these same landed families usually have quite sizeable art collections.'

'Investments. Outward symbols of their wealth and position,' Wayne scoffed. 'Civilised people have to have certain cultural standards. In reality they despise artists. Leigh's father never let an opportunity go by that he didn't attempt to ridicule me under the guise of having a bit of fun!'

'Then why allow them to make you feel guilty or inadequate for their limitations? A very large section of the world reveres its artists. If others question what they're all about, it means they've failed to achieve their own cultural growth. I guess we have to be secure in our own identity. It doesn't come easily. There are so many conflicts, so many rough patches to iron out.'

'You're a person though, aren't you?' Wayne took her hand. 'A real person. You're not an extension of some peer group. You have a fine appreciation of so many things. An understanding. I found you tremendously sympathetic at our first meeting. That's largely why I agreed to do the interview. Some interviewers are so trite, so pushy they alienate me right off. You didn't. You understand fantasy and feeling. You understand an artist's inner life.' He leaned over and pressed an ardent kiss on her cheek, a gesture complicated by Guy Trenton's casual witness.

Leigh, absorbed in him as she was, followed his gaze and Sara, seized by an imp of mischief, gave them a frivolous little wave.

'Make the perfect couple, don't they?' Wayne observed almost mournfully.

'I don't know that I've met the perfect couple,' Sara returned candidly. 'I've met plenty of lords and kings.'

'Is that a dig at Trenton?' Wayne suddenly grinned at her.

'I guess it is. Perhaps unfair. I don't know the man.'

'My dear, the assumption is as soon as Guy Trenton wants anything he gets it. He very nearly runs this part of the world. If that's not being lordly I don't know what is. It's nothing for him to pay millions for a property. You'd think Trenton Estates would be enough to work on, but he goes from one project to another. For practical purposes you could say he's in everything. He's only got to whisper and it reaches the State capital. Likely as not they'll knight him in another ten years.'

'Knighthoods don't bypass artists,' Sara told him lightly. 'Didn't you mention how much you admired Sir Sydney Nolan's work in our interview?'

Wayne smiled and shrugged. 'I'll never rise so high.'

Sara secured her seat-belt, checking the impulse to question Wayne's attitude. Could one ever accomplish great things without aiming for the stars? Being ambitious was central to success. She liked Wayne. She admired his work and she wanted to understand him better. Oddly, it occurred to her that he could do with a dollop of Guy Trenton's fire, which wasn't exactly what she wanted to think. Trenton was a man committed to a high destiny. He was super-confident with a mind to match the dynamic image. Sara was aware Wayne had problems. He wasn't a man who would be at home anywhere, as Trenton was, but there was sweetness and sensitivity in his thin, attractive face, a quick intelligence in his eyes. He wasn't the kind of man to box a woman into a corner and keep her there. Or so, at this stage of their relationship, Sara interpreted his character.

The Piper's engines sputtered then roared into life. Given clearance, the pilot taxied down the runway, gathering speed for the lift-off. The noise level was above anything Sara was used to, but that scarcely accounted for her curious feeling of uneasy awareness, almost like a premonition.

'Nothing for you to worry about.' Wayne reached over and caught her hand.

'You don't have storms, do you, at this time of the year?' she asked jokingly.

'It's possible, but the pilot knows his job.'

'In that case let's relax and enjoy our little jaunt. Two weeks in Paradise is just the right therapy to help me reorganise my life.'

'Mine was a muddle until I met you,' Wayne told her softly. 'You're so vital! You could bring a man out of uncertainty and desperation.'

Surely that was something a man should do himself?

If Sara frowned slightly, Wayne didn't notice. He tightened his grip on her hand sighing deeply. 'This is where I live and this is what I am. I'm going to paint a portrait of you so beautiful it's going to take your breath away.'

'I'm honoured,' Sara said sincerely though her green eyes were slightly wary. Wayne had never spoken to her so intensely before. She realised, of course, that he was interested in her as she was interested in him, but she didn't want to be hurried into something she wasn't ready for. She had come to please him and further their friendship.

She didn't know then what she was letting herself in for.

CHAPTER TWO

FORTY minutes out the sky had darkened and Sara couldn't deceive herself that she wasn't feeling just that little bit afraid.

Guy Trenton got up and manoeuvred his way back to them, his golden gaze searching Sara's pale face. 'How's it going back here?'

'Fine. The time passes swiftly,' Wayne assured him. 'Sara?'

'I'll be pleased when we've landed,' she admitted frankly.

'You could do up your seat-belt,' he suggested. 'It's always a good idea to stay strapped in. We could strike a little turbulence. The warning light will come on in any case.'

Sara obeyed instantly but Wayne, unexpectedly, voiced his objection. 'I've flown through a lot worse than this.'

'Maybe you have,' Guy Trenton agreed mildly, 'but you know as well as I how unpredictable the air over the jungle can be. It's senseless to take any risks. There's fairly thick cloud ahead, and the plane could do some bouncing around.'

'I do hope I've the good grace not to be sick,' Sara joked wryly.

'We'll make it,' he smiled at her and his smile was filled with such confidence that Sara, despite herself, felt better. 'Just sit back and relax.'

'You'd think we didn't know to do up our seat-belts ourselves,' Wayne muttered resentfully.

'I think he was only offering reassurance.' Sara looked out of the window at the increasingly thick

26

cloud. 'How extraordinary that we could come from clear skies to this!'

'You're in the tropics now, Sara.' Wayne's brown eyes reflected Sara's anxiety. Now the clouds were full of rain and the plane went into a series of sickening little lurches as it battled against the whirling masses of energy.

Sara pushed back stiffly into her seat, her hands clutching the edge of it as the plane seemed to drop perpendicularly before bouncing up again. Even the engines were whining and just as Sara began to pray they would ride it out lightning struck in a vivid flash, burying its bolt in the fuselage and disabling the plane's electrical system.

'My God, we've been struck!' Wayne shouted above the explosive crack.

It's not possible, Sara thought. It's not possible we're going to die. Instead of hysteria, she experienced a violent determination to stay alive. She wasn't ready yet to surrender her young life.

They were losing height rapidly. She knew that from the sickening plunge and the build-up of pressure in her ears. She swallowed convulsively, turning her head the better to absorb what was happening to them. Wayne had his eyes tightly closed, his head pressed back against the seat, his whole body straining. Up ahead of them Leigh Sutton was framed in shock, her eyes wide open, while Guy Trenton had somehow worked his way into the co-pilot's seat. She thought that would have to be the way of it. It was outside his experience not to *act*.

They were gliding. Incredibly, now they were out of the thick cloud it was absolutely still. There were trees beneath them. Not trees in a vast open field, but trees so thick an army could have marched across them. The canopy looked completely closed, with great patches of colour embroidering the deep emerald carpet. The trees were in flower. Blossoms to decorate their graves.

Someone was crying wildly. Sara brought her hand up to her throat, unsure in these crazed moments where the sound was coming from. Her vocal chords were still. These were the strangest moments she had ever experienced in her life. When she should have been full of fear she dared to keep up hope. Was it mankind's deepest instinct, or was she traumatised?

They hit the trees with a shocking crash. Disaster seemed inevitable, yet somehow they continued on their swift, bumpy ride, shearing off branches as they went. Rain was falling outside and the plane was screeching, jerking, cracking yet fighting against being torn apart. They were almost skipping across the trees, much as a stone does across water, while the two men fought to keep the wings level and the nose up.

She went in. Further and further into the jungle until the plane stopped as if it had come up against a brick wall. Sara felt the snapping pain right through her body then a moment later the plane took a nose-dive, sinking at a sickening angle through a glowing patch of trees.

A woman screamed in terror and Sara slumped forward bending her body and averting her face for the moment when the plane would crash through the trees and burst into flame. There was another sudden downward jolt, then miraculously they were caught and held in a brace of strangler figs heavily covered with ferns and mosses and lichens. It was almost as if they were enclosed in a giant flowering basket, and Sara lifted her head in absolute wonderment. Was it possible they were to survive?

Predictably it was Guy Trenton who made the first move. He released the pilot, Jake, from his harness, checking the wound on his right temple from where blood was trickling. Sara could see the pilot's head was slack and she forgot about the danger that was threatening, unbuckled herself and stood up.

Wayne was still sitting numbly and Leigh Sutton's cries of terror had given way to a dull sobbing.

'Move slowly,' Guy Trenton cautioned her.

'Is he badly hurt?'

'Concussed. He's bleeding from the temple. We have to get out of here as quickly as possible.' His face was formidable in its striking concentration. 'Palmer?' He looked past Sara to where Wayne was slumped over, then when he realised Wayne was in shock the timbre of his voice cracked. *'Palmer?'* It worked. Wayne lifted his head. 'Pull yourself together, man. We mightn't stay aloft too much longer. Jake here is concussed, how badly I don't know. You'll have to get the women out. Go down through the trees. It won't be too difficult. There'll be plenty to cling to. The trees are covered with stout ferns and vines.'

'My God!' Wayne was spluttering, obviously trying to regain his balance and confidence.

'What about you?' Sara looked to Guy Trenton urgently. 'How are you going to manage? That poor man is only barely conscious. You'll have to support him all the way.'

'I'll manage.' He held up an authoritative hand as Sara went to move nearer. 'Stay where you are. You're to move as slowly and evenly as possible. Try and calm Leigh.'

'Leigh, please, I beg of you,' Sara put her hand on the older girl's shoulder. 'We're safe and we can get out of here.'

'Safe? Incredible!' Leigh gave a wild laugh. 'We don't know yet that we won't be killed.'

'You might be if you're going to sit there much longer.' Sara bent closer and stared into the girl's eyes. 'Come, I'll help you.'

'How? How can *you* help me?' Leigh protested violently. 'You know nothing about the jungle. There are pythons all around us.'

'If there are, they'll get out of your way.' Guy Trenton with the pilot slumped against him started forward. 'We haven't time for histrionics, Leigh. I have an injured man here. I want to get you all safely out of the way, then I'm going to try to salvage as much as I can from the aircraft. We've lost all radio contact.'

'Stand up, Leigh,' Sara said firmly, unbuckling the other girl's harness. 'It would be terrible to be alone, but we're all together.'

'Don't worry, Leigh, only the good die young,' Wayne suddenly said, his voice dry and brittle.

It gave Leigh a flash of her characteristic super-confidence. 'I think you'd better go first and prepare the way,' she taunted him, 'though playing the hero isn't your style.'

'If we're going to fight among ourselves it's going to increase our problems,' Guy Trenton told them quietly. 'Go on, Wayne. Open the door. You climbed enough trees when you were a boy.'

In the shock of their forced landing Sara had disregarded the fact that she had struck her head. Now it began to pound painfully.

'Are you all right?' Guy Trenton asked her sharply.

'I'm in great shape. Lucky to be alive.'

'You're as white as a sheet. Stay close to me.'

'I intend to. You might need help.'

Yet she made no contribution. The pilot seemed to have passed out and, though he was a compact man of medium height, Guy Trenton slung him over his shoulder as though he were little more than a skeleton.

'Get moving, girl.'

Sara felt tremors of fear running through her body, but she recovered enough to step out on to a vine-wreathed branch. The height from the ground stopped

her short for a moment but the tree was dense with
hand and foot holds and great dangling lianas like
monkey-ropes. Even in the midst of disaster she
couldn't help thinking of a recent movie she had seen.
The Lord of the Jungle had flourished in such a
setting, travelling at almost tree-top level by way of
these vines. She looked back and saw Guy Trenton
climbing strongly. Even in the midst of total confusion she was stirred by his strength and mind
control. If he lost his footing he would most probably
fall on her. The thought even made her half lose her
balance.

There was no sign of Wayne or Leigh. Then she
saw them vaulting multiple prop roots and running
swiftly. Oh my God, surely Guy Trenton would need
help? She could never have run, even if it meant losing
her own life.

She almost fell towards the bottom and Guy
Trenton grabbed her with his free arm, pulling her
against him with bruising strength. 'Stay here,' he ordered. 'Where the hell is Palmer?'

'They've run. I guess they're frightened.'

He cursed violently beneath his breath. 'That's a
big help.'

'I can jump,' Sara muttered. 'Don't worry about
me. I'll slide, then I'll jump.'

'You'll never take Jake's weight.' He looked about
him trying to think what he could use. 'Can you grab
that vine?'

'Leave it to me,' Sara started towards a thick, dangling woody vine. Her hand brushed against something and she recoiled so violently she almost fell.

'Sara, for God's sake, get on with it.'

'That was a snake.'

'It's not bothering you, is it?'

She swallowed in horror. 'I guess not.' She reached
out and hooked the vine around her arm. She didn't
know it, but tears were running down her face.

'Good girl!' He took it in his hand, wrenching hard to test its strength. 'I'll make it up to you. We'll get out of here. Trust me.'

She stared at him, shuddering repeatedly. Though her mind was responding well to danger, her body was reacting. She could never imagine him running, giving up. Another minute more and he was showing her how Tarzan did it, flying down through the trees to a small clearing. The impetus thrust him roughly back against a tree trunk, but he continued to hold the pilot, shielding him with his body.

Sara felt an enormous surge of relief and decided to move.

'Jump, Sara,' he called. 'I'll catch you.'

She summoned up the courage to let go, for terrifying seconds dropping like a stone until his arms came up and he deftly caught her, pivoting, never stumbling until he slowed down enough to jerk her upright. She was dimly aware of some queer excitement but it was all wrong.

'Now, run!'

'Don't be crazy, I'm not going to leave you.'

'*Run!*' He almost flung her towards a giant fern.

'You bastard!' Incredibly she charged him flailing with her fist. 'I can handle this as well as you can.'

'Good for you.' He caught her wrist above her head. 'If you don't care about getting killed we can use your strength to better advantage. We've got to get as far away from the plane as possible until I'm sure it's not going to blow.'

'Right!' The intense anger she felt at him changed. 'I'll get on Jake's other side.'

'What you *can* do is lead the way.'

'Yes, boss.' She dived away while he picked up the pilot and once again hoisted him on his shoulder.

A branch whipped back on her, half knocking the breath from her. There were no recognisable tracks, only an incredibly lush forest of great vaulting trees like pillars and masses and masses of intertwining and climbing vines. The floor of the forest was a thick bed of ferns, velvety mosses and small flowering plants. Every tree was festooned with epiphytes of all kinds: monster staghorns, climbing orchids with strongly scented cascading sprays and some plant that took the form of large bunches of white flowers all up the trunk and the branches. It was fabulous, and she felt she had to be half dreaming. How could anyone suffer a plane crash, yet almost immediately become enchanted by the wilderness? She glanced behind quickly but he was solidly there. The mere turn of her head earned her a slash in the face, but so much adrenalin was flowing it was a miracle just to be safe.

He didn't call a halt until they were some few hundred yards away and the giant ferns had begun to thin. There was a clear patch ahead like a stage setting illuminated by dazzling shafts of light. The rain had poured through the forest canopy for every leaf, every flower, every great frond was ablaze with diamonds and crystal puddles of rain water were cupped by the giant plants.

Guy Trenton lowered the pilot to the ground, his eyes settling on Sara's wildly dishevelled appearance. Her hair in the humid heat was a wild riot of curls thick with leaves like chunks of emeralds. Her silk blouse and slacks were rent in places and stained with green and black streaks. Even her porcelain skin was smeared with green, and there was a trickle of blood from her hairline.

'You look wildly primitive, Miss Richardson,' he said.

'How is one supposed to look in the middle of the jungle? Are you all right?'

'Of course.' He made a self-dismissing gesture. 'God knows what's wrong with Jake. He's badly concussed, that's for sure.' He had propped the pilot into a sitting position with his head slumped to one side.

Now he began to moan and even scuffed at the decayed layer of leaves with his shoe.

'He's coming around,' Sara said hopefully and went to the pilot's side. 'There'll be a first-aid kit in the plane. We should get it.'

'I'll have to wait until I'm sure the plane won't blow up. I think if it was going to it would have by now. The fuel lines were shut off and the fuselage is remarkably intact. Someone up there loves us.'

Jake was muttering and Guy Trenton bent lower. 'Take it easy, Jake. We're OK.'

'Leave me. Save yourselves.'

'No one is leaving anyone. We all stick together.'

'Would you like a drink, Jake?' Sara pounced on a big circular leaf, its centre full of rain water.

'Marvellous!' Jake sighed groggily. Sara made a funnel of the leaf and poured the cold water into his mouth. He drank greedily and afterwards had the strength to smile at her. 'I sure picked up the right passenger. The hell of it is, I picked the wrong cloud.'

'You can't blame yourself for that,' Sara told him. 'That lightning came right at us.'

'Reckon I didn't do too well,' Jake groaned unhappily. 'It was Mr Trenton here flew the plane in those last moments. He's the one who landed us safely. I couldna done half so well.'

'Don't talk, Jake. Save your strength,' Guy Trenton advised him. 'I'll wait a while longer then I'll make a few forays to the plane. At the moment it's held in a brace, but it could crash through to the ground.'

'I'll come with you,' Sara offered.

'You'll stay with Jake.'

'It will save a lot of time if I come with you,' Sara said, tilting her chin high.

'Where's Palmer, the girl?' Jake looked around in a kind of protest.

'I guess they're still running,' Sara said wryly.

'And so would you be if you had any sense,' Guy Trenton told her. 'The man who gets you will have his hands full.'

'There aren't enough good men around.' Sara's green eyes flashed. 'What do you think, Jake, would the plane have blown up by now if it was going to?'

'I'm totally against taking you,' Guy Trenton interrupted.

'And for God's sake, what would we do if *you* got killed?'

'I was rather hoping Palmer would return.'

'One would think so.' Sara bit her lip, perplexed. 'Probably he thought his first duty was to save Leigh.'

'Incredible that he forgot *you*.'

There was no way she could get around that one.

They sat for another half-hour, then Guy Trenton stood up, cupped his hands and sent a bushman's coo-ee echoing through the forest. The echo bounded from tree to tree and now Sara saw the trees were alive with birds. While she watched astounded they burst into flight, legion upon legion, their brilliant colours everywhere: blue, green, red, aqua, purple and the most intense golden yellow. They picked up Guy Trenton's call in full chorus almost drowning out all other sound.

'Palmer, can you hear me?'

'Maybe he hurt himself jumping from the tree,' Jake suggested dispiritedly.

'He didn't hurt himself, I saw them running,' Sara confirmed. 'They would be tired. They would have to rest.'

'Hang on,' Guy Trenton ordered. 'That's someone.'

Sara couldn't hear anything. Still...

An answering coo-ee floated across the forest arches. The wilderness had swallowed them up but Guy Trenton continued to call until about forty feet away Wayne and Leigh emerged from the undergrowth of shrubs and made their way towards them.

Wayne had his arm around Leigh's waist, both of them unnervingly tattered and scratched.

'Thank God you're safe,' Guy Trenton called reassuringly. 'Now we're all together, I'm sure we can strip the plane of whatever we want.'

Wayne was slow to respond, or he was so much in shock he hadn't heard.

'Wayne?' Sara ran forward rather desperately, staring into his face. 'Let me take care of Leigh. Guy wants to go back to the plane.'

'Now?' Wayne was trembling violently. 'Don't you know it could blow up?'

'Guy doesn't think it will.' Sara put her hand on his hand, a gesture of support and comfort. 'Don't you see, you have to help him?'

'What are you talking about, Sara?' he stared at her. 'I don't want to die. Surely you know that.'

'We're going to die anyway,' Leigh said in a gasping voice. 'We were blown off course. We have no radio. We're cut off from the rest of the world. Who would know where to look?'

Jake staggered to his feet, his forehead creased with pain. 'They'll find us, Miss Sutton. Mr Trenton here was able to get out a call.'

'Did you? *Did* you, Guy?' Leigh almost pitched towards him and he caught her in his strong arms.

'We're going to be all right, Leigh,' he told her though he looked very angry and formidable. 'I'm convinced I could get out of here even without a search party. My main concern is to get whatever I can from the plane. Jake is in pain and the rest of us are covered in scratches. They need attention.'

'I'll come with you,' Jake muttered, gritting his teeth.

'You can't, Jake,' Sara said furiously, 'you look ill. Damn it, Wayne, can't you go?'

'Have you no concept of how dangerous it is?' Wayne shouted grimly. 'The plane could crash through the trees. It's too much to ask.'

'Guy is pretty sure it will hold.'

'Then let Guy go.' Leigh gave a hysterical laugh. 'Can you imagine what it would be like if they were both killed? Our pilot is half dead already and so he should be. It's all his fault!'

'Why don't you shut up,' Sara said curtly.

'It's all *his* fault,' Leigh repeated wildly. 'Get away from me.'

'I want you all to stay here,' Guy Trenton ordered coldly as though he recoiled from the collective hysteria. If you break away, Leigh, Wayne, I promise you, you'll get lost.'

Wayne shook his tousled head. 'We're not going any place.'

Without another thought in her head Sara turned and ran after Guy Trenton. 'If I want to kill myself that's my business,' she told him emotionally. 'You need help.'

'I don't need a woman's life on my hands.' He turned and caught her by the shoulders, his golden eyes narrowed to mere slits. 'I don't doubt your courage, Sara, but stay shy of that plane. I'll get to it a dozen times if I have to and I'll do it without a hitch. I can't take my mind off the job to worry about you.'

'You'd have let Wayne help you.'

'He's a man,' he said quietly.

'So what's wrong with a woman? Are you eliminating me because of my sex?'

He lifted a hand and cupped her chin. 'I'm eliminating you because I couldn't bear to think of you all blown to pieces.'

She had to jog to catch up with him. 'There's something wrong here. You said you were pretty sure the plane was safe. Were you only saying that to make us feel good?'

'Sara, stop talking. Go back to the others.'

'No chance. I'll wait here, seeing you're so adamant, but the minute you've got everything out I'm coming in to take what I can carry. Maybe the others will lend a hand as soon as they feel a twinge of guilt.'

'I wouldn't bet on that.'

'In that case, take care.' She stopped suddenly, the sting of tears behind her eyes. She was astonished at the force of her admiration for him, so powerful it overcame her instinctive feelings of animosity.

'Damn right.' His shapely mouth twisted into a mocking grin. 'You're quite a girl, Sara, even if you do have a few kinky bits that worry me.'

'So you noticed? And while we're being so honest, I don't accept male supremacy as the natural law.'

'And who in particular made you feel so helpless?'

'I'm not telling. Probably not ever.'

'You're a tough kid!' He suddenly caught hold of her and arched her back over his arm. 'Weren't the knights of old sent off to battle with a kiss?'

'Only by someone who loved them.' She seemed to be having trouble breathing.

'How many men have *you* kissed you didn't love?'

'Trenton,' she said warningly, 'you let me go.'

His golden eyes mocked her. 'You know what it is, Sara? You're so angry at men you can't really love them. You need help. What do you say we stay up all night talking about it?'

'How can you fool at a time like this?'

'Who's fooling?' he asked abruptly and lowered his eyes to her luscious mouth. 'What's Palmer to you?'

'We're good friends. Getting to be good friends.'

'What, you go to football games together?'

'Let me go, Trenton,' she gritted, aware she was almost panting through her half-open mouth.

'Easy, little filly,' he laughed gently and pulled her close. 'Is it possible you're experiencing something you don't want to?'

'All right, kiss me,' she dared him furiously, biting down hard on her nether lip.

He bent to her as though he was catching her woman fragrance, lifted his head back slightly and excitement leapt all the way into her throat. It almost choked her.

'Damn you, *no*!' She felt a kind of terrible inevitability then the absolute mastery of his kiss swept everything else aside. She was devastated. *Branded* by the imprint of his mouth on hers.

'You must be mad . . . *mad*!' she heard herself muttering incoherently, her breasts crushed against the hard wall of his chest, their fused bodies generating a stunning, glowing heat. His virility was such a force it was an assault on her very core. Her very limbs were paralysed. She had feared his power from the very first moment. Now she *knew* he had power over her.

It was central to her emotional dilemma, and Sara dragged her mouth away violently, all her resistance to domination come alive. Her eyes were so tightly shut she couldn't see that he, too, looked strung up and taut, a faint pallor beneath his golden skin. If he had got to her, maybe she had got to him.

'You're an intense creature, aren't you?' he challenged her in a deep, stalking voice.

Who was *he* to talk of intensity after inflicting so much torture? 'So are you!'

'I only wanted a kiss, Sara, not a conflagration.'

'Then might I point out you shouldn't allow a conflagration to develop?' Her mouth was pulsing, probably bruised.

'Red hair!' He wound a long curling strand around his finger. 'That kiss will haunt me.'

'I'll have forgotten it by the time you get back.'

'Typical cover-up, darling,' he smiled at her. 'You're scared silly of what we shared.' He saluted her and began to move off purposefully.

'You take care, do you hear me?' she shouted after him. 'Take care.' Robbed of all strength, she sank to the ground.

Night fell with incredible swiftness. One moment a soft mauve mist swirled down from the tops of the trees, the next they were enveloped in a darkness so black Sara would have been deeply disturbed, had it not been for the comfort of a fire. It was considerably cooler and she was glad of the protection of her jacket. Guy Trenton had made several forays to the plane and each time returned with something practical and useful, not the least a machete and a rifle. Single-handedly he had cleared the way, and now they were camped at the base of a monumental forest giant whose great buttresses formed natural caves.

Sara had done her best to clean up Jake Lewin's head wound, watching him anxiously as he swallowed a couple of pain-killers. He was far too groggy for her liking, his lucid moments further and further apart. The wound didn't look all that bad, but obviously it had caused a depression in a vital spot. She knew Guy Trenton shared her anxiety even if Leigh was nearly snarling with rage and fear and Wayne's morale had almost collapsed.

'My God, what's that?' Leigh cried stridently as something in the forest crashed to the ground.

'Move back further into the tree, Leigh,' Guy Trenton advised her quietly. 'Debris is always crashing to the ground in the jungle. Most of the animals are out of their hiding-places. This is the time they hunt for food. That was probably a branch some ringtail possum dislodged.'

'I'm hungry,' Leigh moaned.

Guy turned his head. 'Give Leigh another piece of chocolate,' he told Sara.

She nodded mutely and moved back to their little pile of supplies. He had thought her responsible at least, for he had placed her in charge of their short line of provisions.

'Why is it *you're* so calm and collected?' Leigh accused her. 'Haven't you the brain to know fear?'

'Who said I wasn't afraid?' Sara sat down beside Wayne and took his thin hand in hers, squeezing hard. 'The crucial factor is whether I can get over the top of it. I believe we'll eventually get out of here.'

'Fantastic!' Leigh laughed and smeared a hand over her badly scratched face. 'Haven't you been taking any notice of what we've been going through? The jungle goes on for ever. Experienced stockmen get lost every day even on the forest fringe.'

'Take notice of the stars,' Guy Trenton said. 'The old mariners followed them. I grew up in Ceylon, but I've learnt a lot about this country. It's possible to get out of here, Leigh. I know what I'm doing. Sara has collected all the rainwater from the leaves and we can always dig for it even if we can't come on a pool or a waterhole. We have water. We have tea and coffee, sugar, milk. We have chocolate, a couple of packets of biscuits and a box of apples. Tomorrow I'll shoot a few birds. We'll cook them like the natives do, in a covered-up hole in the ground.'

'Yuck!' Leigh groaned.

'You'll simply have to make the best of it,' Guy told her. 'Anyway, cooked that way they're delicious. The fruits and the plant matter in the forest sustain all animal life. They can sustain us for the relatively short time it will take us to reach some station outpost. The authorities will know by now when and where we disappeared.'

'We're off-course.' Wayne seemed very grateful for Sara's hand.

'They'll know that too.' Guy Trenton bent his strong, striking face nearer the fire. Skin and eyes shone like copper, his thick, curling hair was like jet. 'There's nothing more for us to do now but try and get some sleep. At first light we'll move. I'm going to try and make a stretcher of sorts for Jake. His condition is deteriorating.'

'What are you going to make it with?' Sara asked.

'There was a small tarpaulin on the plane. We have rugs, pillows, any amount of timber. It'll be simple.'

'And to attach it?'

'I've got rope.'

Sara remembered now he had returned with it, coiled over his shoulder. 'I'll take the first spell.'

'Spell of what?' The faintest mocking laugh emanated from his lean throat.

'Doesn't somebody have to watch the fire?' she returned spiritedly. 'We might have a few unwelcome visitors.'

'Visitors?' Leigh gave a laugh as sharp as a bird's.

'I think Sara means wallabies and the like,' Guy said in a matter-of-fact voice. 'The possums won't come near us. The snakes are after birds and the owls will take care of any tree rodents.' He didn't mention the countless large frogs that would be hopping around fresh from their day's burrowing in the moist soil of the rain-forest. Nor did he talk about the great amethyst pythons that strangled wallabies in their coils. Even the giant yellow spotted goannas, second only to the fearsome Indonesian monitor, the Komodo dragon, foraged in the monsoon forests. At least it hunted by day, but its sudden appearance could be frightening.

'You've cleared this out properly, haven't you, Guy?' Leigh wailed. She was referring to the cave-like buttresses of the rain-forest giant, home to unspeakable things like spiders and stinging ants.

Perhaps she ought to try doing something herself, Sara thought, but Guy was incredibly gentle with her. He stood up, unfolding lithely to his full daunting height and went to her, rearranging the rug that had been allotted to her inside the semi-enclosed space and plumping up the small cabin pillow. 'There's Valium. I don't think it would hurt if you took one. Better to sleep out the shock.' Splendid as he was in his own physical and mental fitness, Sara was pleased and surprised to see he was sympathetic towards those much weaker than himself.

Leigh, too, reacted with her first wavering smile. 'I'm in awe of you, Guy, sometimes. In a way you're as aloof from the rest of us as this jungle. It must make you feel very contemptuous of frail women like me.'

'Never.' He put out a hand and smoothed her tangled hair. 'You've had to contend with a great deal these past hours. Recognise it and take it easy on yourself. We might never be able to laugh about this, but at least it will make a good after-dinner story.'

'Perhaps I ought to have one too.' Wayne's slanted brown eyes were etched in with dark shadows.

'What's that, Wayne?'' Guy swung about, studying the younger man sitting beside Sara on a moss-covered log.

'A Valium,' Wayne said slowly. 'You probably haven't had a headache in your life, but I suffer frightful migraines.'

'You haven't got one coming on, have you?' Sara asked almost sharply. Someone had to help Guy Trenton carry the pilot.

'Mercifully, no.' He gazed at Sara with such a hurt expression she had to make an effort to control her feelings.

'I'll get them for you. And Leigh.' She could just see the pale outline of Leigh's face, framed in a dark tangle of hair. 'Try to swallow them with as little water as you can.'

'Are you really so tough?' Leigh taunted her. 'Or are you trying to put on an act for Guy?'

'Leigh, don't you think it would be better if we tried to be friends?' Sara bent down to the other girl with the white tablet in the palm of her hand. 'In my opinion we women ought to stick together. I know you've decided to dislike me on sight, but we're trapped now in a very difficult situation. We have to trust one another and prove to the men we can cope.'

'No matter if we *can't*?' Leigh plucked the tablet out of Sara's hand so excitedly she almost dropped it. 'I don't know what the extent of *your* jungle training is, but even if we get out of here, it's going to be hell.''

'Try to sleep,' Sara said soothingly. 'By morning we'll have adjusted to survival.'

Wayne swallowed his tablet almost as avidly as Leigh, and Sara reflected almost sadly that the differences between him and Guy Trenton could hardly have been more painfully marked. Given the one man was an artist and a loner, the other a man of action, Wayne's limitations were vastly magnified by this primitive environment. He seemed totally incapable of forceful action, whereas Guy Trenton was completely in his element, his exotic appearance in total harmony with the lush jungle.

'Put your rug beside mine,' Wayne begged her. 'I won't be able to sleep unless I know you're safe beside me.'

Sara didn't have the heart to point out that only a few hours before he had been shockingly indifferent to her plight, but then, she reasoned, fear took people differently. Wayne and Leigh had rightly been in terror of their lives. The plane could and perhaps should have blown up. Why should she blame him because he had shown no great heroism? Nevertheless, her early feeling for him was already becoming tarnished. In repudiating a man's dominance and authority, might she not be repudiating the quintessential male? Her present aggressions were an indication of what she had suffered as a helpless child. Maybe her image of men was all wrong. They couldn't all be as bad as her father, yet she had been surrounded by men who only looked on women as objects. It was extremely depressing.

She allowed Wayne to arrange a rug and a groundsheet side by side, but she refused to lie down. Jake was having one of his lucid periods, his forehead resting on his updrawn knees, while Guy Trenton stood over him, realising, from what few questions he was asking, that Jake had difficulty in answering.

'How is he?' Sara asked quietly. 'Jake?' She knelt and touched the pilot's shoulder.

To her surprise he lifted his head and smiled at her. 'I'll come good again. Don't worry.'

'Guy is going to make a stretcher for you.'

He seemed puzzled and gave a wincing frown. 'Mr Trenton shouldn't bother. I'll feel better by the morning.'

His altered appearance even in such a short time horrified Sara. 'Why don't you lie down now and I'll try to make you comfortable.'

'Might be best.' He lay back and Guy Trenton shoved a small cabin pillow beneath his head.

'He can have mine,' Sara said, 'in case he rolls. I don't need a pillow.' She looked over towards her rug and saw to her amazement that Wayne appeared to be deeply asleep. She couldn't imagine falling asleep so quickly in such an alien world and without making plans for the morning. Instead of dangerous times, they might almost have been camping.

'Why don't you try and get some rest now, Sara?' Guy Trenton asked after they had settled the pilot.

'I don't feel in the least able to sleep,' she answered him, disgusted that she wasn't able to control an involuntary dry sob. 'I'm really worried about Jake. We won't be able to go very fast or far if we have to carry him.'

'Then you'll have to stay while I go for help.'

'I imagine that would be just as bad. Wayne's not at his best in this kind of situation and Leigh has led a very comfortable life. She's shocked and afraid. Without you we might go to pieces. There has to be some other way.'

He took her arm and guided her nearer the fire. 'Let's see if Jake does show some improvement first. It's hard to tell if it's a bad concussion or something worse. It might take a few days to restore him to normal function. His visual acuity is good, which doesn't seem to point to a severe lesion. Obviously he's feeling he's somehow to blame, which could put him into deep shock. I'm only guessing. I'm not a medical man.'

'Well, he's suffered some trauma to the head. He doesn't appear to have been injured all that seriously, yet he's getting worse.'

'Could be reaction.'

It seemed obvious he wanted her to leave it at that so Sara sank down near the fire and after a moment he joined her, lean and hard to her supple yielding.

'You'd get out of this pretty quickly, wouldn't you, if you didn't have us?'

He gave her a brief, mocking glance and threw another small branch on the fire. 'Maybe the last thing I would ever have thought of was to crash, but I wanted to get to know you.'

'What for?' Her voice sounded stunned.

'Well.' He smiled and leaned back on his arm. 'You're a fabulous-looking creature. Perhaps a bit tall . . .'

'I'm not that tall,' she started to protest, then she saw that he was teasing. 'Anyway, you'd look ridiculous with a small woman. Are you married?'

'No.'

She shook her red-gold head. 'No, you don't look married. In fact you don't even look tame.'

'Both of us.'

'Both of us what?'

'You don't look tame either, Sara Richardson, and I find myself wondering who I remind you of.' He sounded intensely interested.

'I'm convinced I've never met anyone like you in my life,' she countered, trying to look impassive when the purr in his voice was like a feather down her spine.

'That smacks of evasion, Sara. I thought you'd be much more honest. I've never had a woman look at me with so much antagonism in her eyes. I suspect your view of me might be coloured by some blighted love affair. It's hard to see it could have been Kirkman. I'd have to be an improvement on him. You're certainly not in love with Palmer. I don't want to sound meddlesome but you might have some trouble there. You met him while you were out on an interview?'

'It's none of your business, but that's true.'

'You felt as though your souls touched?'

'You're right about one thing.' Her green eyes glowed like a cat's. 'I disliked you on sight.'

'Because I seared some sensitive spot. In one day I've met Kirkman and Palmer, both of them drawn to Titian hair, green eyes and magnolia skin, so what other intolerable male tried to control you, body and mind?'

'You're crazy.'

'Tell me.'

'Why, because the night is long and something just jumped over my foot?'

'So you noticed?' he laughed. 'I'm glad you're not shocked by little things like frogs.'

She shuddered. 'Actually I'm doing my best to be brave.' Sara drew up her legs.

'You're brave, Sara,' he said drily. 'But you've got a problem, and all because of some *man*.'

'You've got a lot of questions ahead of you before you'll get any answers.'

'So why don't we start at the beginning?' His brilliant eyes raked over her vivid face and slender body. 'How old are you, Sara?'

'I was born in 1609,' she returned lightly. 'This is my third reincarnation.'

'The first time they burnt you as a witch?'

She forgot she was supposed to be dispassionate. 'Women have always been persecuted, haven't they?' She stared into the orange flames. 'More harshly judged than men?'

'No thinking man would deny it,' he returned in an unexpectedly sympathetic voice. 'You don't have to get passionately aggressive with me, Sara. I'm already persuaded.'

'In theory,' she said curtly. 'Not in practice. A woman would only have to look at you to know you would quickly reduce her to a slave.'

'On the basis of my general appearance?' He sounded more sceptical than offended.

'You're the quintessential male. A conqueror by your very nature.'

'Sara, darling,' he finally groaned. 'This is more serious than I thought!'

'I'm not your darling,' she enjoyed telling him. 'In fact I could equally well say I'm no man's darling.'

'You must be!' He leaned back on his elbow again, staring with amused mockery into her face. 'You've picked up not one, not two, but *three* admirers in the one day. Count me in. We really should include Jake as well. You don't look the sort of girl to tell a lie. Even in the short time I've known you, you've shown yourself to be amazingly spunky and difficult to control. You have a father? Doesn't he adore you? So radiant and tender, the richness of that hair! I feel your father must be allowed to call you "darling"?'

'You haven't met my father,' she responded heatedly, rising to his mockery. 'He's a brilliant QC.'

'No!' His gleaming eyes were fixed on her flushed face. 'I happen to recall a Miles Richardson. Would he be any relation?'

'Where did you meet him?' It was Sara's turn to be astonished.

'Not quite so fast. Miles Richardson *is* your father?' His eyes, extremely alert and intelligent, locked hers unwaveringly.

'Indeed he is.' Sara did her very best not to speak bleakly. Unhappy as she had often been, she had never been tempted to discuss her father with anyone outside her mother and that detestable psychiatrist. Even battered children were intensely loyal to their parents.

'Well...' He stroked his lean jaw exploratively. 'You have a very distinguished parent. Your father has an impressive reputation. Does that torment you?'

'What do you mean?' She had to keep her voice from shaking. 'I'm proud of my father's ability.'

'Are you?'

'For God's sake, Trenton, what are you about?'

'Forgive me, Sara.' He shielded his brilliant eyes with narrowed lids. 'Perhaps I'm trying to unravel you too quickly. I met your father at a dinner given in Sir Peter Beechey's honour. An all-male affair. I recall I thought your father would probably be at his very best in such circumstances. He's a marvellous conversationalist, very witty and controversial in the sense he loves a good debate.'

'I expect you took to one another instantly.'

'At least he was a damned good dinner companion. The professional persona is very much to the fore. One finds that a lot with the legal profession. They tend to sum up what the rest of us have to say. Very obviously you take after your mother.'

'My mother is a very special woman, very beautiful and gentle. Perhaps too gentle, too sensitive to cope with being continually in the dock.'

'Sara!'

Immediately she wavered. 'Sorry! I didn't mean to say that. It's the night and the forest. The two of us murmuring beside a fire, seemingly not the least concerned we're hopelessly lost.'

'We're not lost,' he said between a jeer and reassurance. 'We just appear to be lost. I'll rescue you, radiant maiden, never fear!'

'It's Jake I'm concerned for. I'm beyond the point of wondering why I'm not shaken to bits, but this place is fantastic! It's like landing in some magic kingdom, somewhere wild and beautiful and secret.'

'So naturally you feel at home here. You're all those things yourself.'

'It's not your plan to seduce me, is it?' She softened her voice but it had a contemptuous ring.

To her annoyance he laughed. 'Why, because I'm drawn to your beauty and spirit? No, Sara Richardson, I've no intention of becoming involved.'

'Just as well, because here's one radical female who doesn't care to get her wings singed.'

'You have more of your father in you than you think, Sara.'

'Perish the thought!'

'Well, how would you describe yourself—gentle, tolerant, submissive? Would you make a passive partner? I think you'd give a very good account of yourself in the dock.'

'And I think you're a trouble-maker, Trenton.' She sprang up swiftly, but instead of letting her go, he uncoiled like a big cat and caught her shoulders.

'I didn't think I'd enjoy having a woman call me "Trenton" in that scathing fashion; instead I'm finding it entertaining.'

'I suggest you let me go.'

'Kiss me goodnight then. That should put an end to it.'

'Really, you ought to be ashamed!' She could see that he was enjoying himself, treating her more like a kitten with its claws out than a full-grown lioness.

'Well, it's taken your mind off the crash,' he told her, unconcerned. He bent his dark head and aimed a chaste kiss on her white temple. 'Don't leave your blanket beside Palmer's, like a good girl.'

'Why is that?' Her green eyes were enormous and highly defiant.

'I'm only trying to be helpful, my dear. You could, if you like, call me Uncle Guy.'

'No one would cast you in the role of "Uncle".'

'Shows what *you'd* know. I'm the doting uncle of three.' To her amazement he walked back and collected her rug, not even sparing a glance for the supine Wayne. 'There now,' he spread the rug out nearer the fire, 'it would be a good idea if you tried to get some rest. I'd like to get going at first light.' He straightened up, his every movement easy, fluid and controlled. 'Come along, Sara, defiant girl. Curl up and see how quickly you can fall off to sleep.'

'So where are *you* going?' She was half-way to the ground when a dark form flapped overhead. 'What the heck is that?'

'Calm. Keep calm.' He pressed her down with a hand on her shoulder. 'Nothing is going to pounce on you while I'm about. That was a flying fox searching for a fruiting tree.'

'In that case I'd like to be undercover like Leigh.'

'Poor Leigh!' he sighed gently. 'The sooner I get you all back to civilisation, the better!'

CHAPTER THREE

THE sweet powerful voice of a bird woke her.

Sara sat bolt upright, fully alert, while the single birdsong began to build, bright whistles and chatterings like a wondrously strange orchestra tuning up. It was dawn in the rain-forest and its unearthly beauty brought an astonishing new dimension into her life. The atmosphere was one of incredible tranquillity, with the ethereal light filtering through the brilliant greens and festooning the magnificent tree ferns in silver. It was nature's great cathedral, and Sara found herself moved in a way she had never been before.

Leaves fell by her ear; fluffy cream blossoms released by the trees. The mixture of scents was marvellously clean and fresh, exquisite in its uniqueness. One bird, the first bird, was clearly the soloist in the forest orchestra. Its voice was bigger, more beautiful, more powerful. It soared about the great gothic pillars and echoed down the verdant aisles. Smaller, harmonious voices poured down, and Sara thought the Garden of Eden must have been like this.

She turned her head and stared around her. Incredibly, the others were still asleep, deaf to the astonishingly loud and spectacular birdsong. Choruses of birds were mimicking others so that at times it sounded like the greatest fugue ever composed. There was no sign of Guy, but this didn't surprise her. He seemed to know instinctively the ways of the forest, and by virtue of his strength and capacity for leadership it had become his charge to lead them out. He would probably be scouting a track now. It didn't even cross her mind that he might have struck out for himself. Such an act would be unthinkable in a man of his calibre. Temporarily at least, every trace of her own deeply driven male-female conflict had been suppressed. Civilisation most probably would set it on the loose again.

Sara moved back quietly to where Jake was lying. Surely his colour was good? She was frightened of touching him in case he needed that extra sleep but she risked brushing the lightest touch over his skin. It was cool. No fever, thank God. She sank down on her knees and whispered a prayer of thanks. It was easy now to believe there was a God watching over them and nowhere did He seem closer than in this awe-inspiring forest.

They had all arranged themselves as best they could by the time Guy Trenton returned. There was no water for washing but at least there were brushes and combs. Jake had cried out once when Sara changed his dressing, but otherwise he was in full possession of himself and had endured a few of Leigh's intolerable remarks in silence. It was certain she was going to hold on to the belief that negligence on Jake's part had caused the crash, and no amount of talk of Acts of God was going to change it.

'A surprise for breakfast!' Guy had a canvas bag half hidden over his shoulder, now he threw it down. He looked rakishly, boldly handsome with his black hair curling riotously and his darkly tanned skin flushed with exertion.

'What is it?' Sara clapped her hands together, fired by his elation.

'Take a look.' He laughed and his fine white teeth were illuminated against his golden skin.

Leigh stood up slowly and walked towards him, but Sara pounced on the canvas bag like a terrier. 'My God!' She looked up, amazed. 'Fish! Are you some kind of magician then?'

Leigh began to laugh almost hysterically. 'Of course he's a magician!' She threw herself at him and his arms closed around her in unfeigned delight. 'Oh, Guy, this means we can be clean!' Leigh, in fact, had doused herself in perfume.

'And fed.' He laughed down at her. 'Now, the sooner we've eaten the sooner we can get on our way. The lagoon is a good six miles away, but the going will be easier this time. I've hacked out a path and marked it.' He put Leigh away gently and walked towards Jake. 'How goes it?'

'A lot better today, Mr Trenton.' Jake rose up from the log he had been sitting on. 'They say sleep is the great mender.'

Guy put his hand on the older man's shoulder, studying him keenly. 'I've made a stretcher for when you feel tired. Understand there's nothing to be achieved by trying too hard. If you start to feel ill, let us know what's happening.'

'I will, boss.' Jake tried to grin. 'I have to thank Sara for seeing to the wound. She'd make a great nurse.'

'How would she be at scaling fish?'

'No problem.' Sara smiled easily at his little taunt.

'I'll do it, Sara,' Wayne offered. This morning he was extremely subdued, silent too at Leigh's little digs. Sara hadn't the least doubt Leigh could be charming under favourable circumstances, but right now she was distinctly unpleasant. Only Guy had been spared the nasty side of her nature.

The fish was delicious. Sara thought she had never tasted such food in her life.

'The main thing to remember,' Guy told them, 'is to keep together. Anyone who wanders off could very easily get lost. Don't eat any fruits or berries without checking with me first. Don't reach out to touch any plants.'

It was very difficult for Sara to follow orders because they were passing through galleries of great staghorn and elkhorn ferns and exquisite, scented orchids growing as epiphytes on trees and rocks. In different places white fleshy fungi decorated the decaying leaves but on either side of the track Guy had beaten the plant life was overwhelmingly dense. Everything was on a gigantic scale and magnificent ferns the size of trees bent their great fronds twenty feet above their heads.

They were tramping noisily and with difficulty when Leigh screamed.

'What is it?' Guy, a bleeding cut across his high cheekbone, swerved.

'Get it off me, *off me*!' Leigh was wailing, her hands moving agitatedly across her hair and face.

Wayne came to her assistance but instead of welcoming him she slapped at his hands. 'It's a cobweb, cobweb and there's something in it.'

In fact a small bird and a once magnificent blue butterfly had been ensnared in the monstrous, near invisible web. Now Leigh's hair was thickly silvered and the wings of the butterfly clung to her designer jeans.

Guy had to calm her and Sara took the minute to dash the blood off his cheekbone with a clean tissue she had stuffed in her pocket. His hands too were a mass of scratches and there was another long bleeding scratch travelling down from his throat to his chest where it disappeared into a dark mat of hair. 'Shouldn't you have antiseptic on those?' She felt he was taking the brunt of it all.

'We'll all clean up when we reach the water.'

'Everyone will have learnt what has happened to us, won't they, Guy?' Leigh begged him.

'They'll know we've crashed and they'll be looking for us by now.' He didn't burden her with the knowledge that their plane would by now be invisible from the air, though someone with experience might mark the damage to the rain-forest's canopy. Even then they could attribute it to the violent storm.

By the time they reached the pool, augmented by storm water, Sara was drenched in sweat and decidedly light-headed. She supposed her queer feeling of unreality must be delayed shock. She had been doing rather well up until now but when she walked into a nest of green tree ants her nerve snapped. Ants ran over her in all directions, so many of them she seemed to sway and stumble backwards as though giving up all effort to hit them off. It almost seemed to her in her reduced state they might carry her off, for they were forming chains like cables and their aggression was remarkable.

'Sara!' Guy was beside her in an instant, his voice taut with anxiety. 'For the love of heaven, girl!' He swatted the insects off, even running his hand into the neck of her blouse. It was a purely practical gesture, but it pulled her together as nothing else could.

'Do you mind!' His hand had covered the swell of her breast.

'Not in the least.' He gave her a devilish grin. 'You girls can take a private dip and I'll try to catch us some crabs for lunch. There should be a few concealed under the rocks.'

'And I hope one of them gives you a good nip.'

'Fire away. That's better.'

The clear mountain stream was one of a chain formed by a tributary of a bigger, fast-flowing river. After their difficult hike, the sight of the emerald-green pool and the two small waterfalls above it was so intoxicating they all pulled off their shoes and ran into the water.

It was cold, very cold, but so clear one could see the bottom.

'This is heaven. *Heaven!*' Sara called. She scooped up handfuls and drank. The almost circular pool was surrounded by great boulders covered in mosses and lichens which strangely seemed to reflect a green light. It was even possible to see flashes of gold as the jungle perch jumped. At the further end, great branches and fronds overhung the water and Guy suggested the girls take their swim first.

Leigh unselfconsciously dived in nude, and Sara, after a moment's hesitation, decided she had better do the same. The men had moved off a little way to allow them privacy and they realised their time was short.

Afterwards, wonderfully refreshed, they dressed behind a screen of ferns then paddled back to the small clearing. 'At least I feel half-way human,' Leigh murmured, 'though I'll never forget this experience until the day I die.'

She was almost companionable as they prepared the lunch of crab meat and apples washed down with tea, and to give them energy for the descent they finished off the chocolate.

'I hope Trenton knows what he's doing,' Wayne grumbled.

'It's logical, surely, to follow the springs to the lowlands.'

'Sure it is,' Wayne agreed shortly. 'But who says we're going in the right direction?'

'He found the first pool, didn't he?' Sara was surprised by Wayne's hostility. 'I don't know about you, but I'd trust him with my life. I *am* trusting him with my life.'

'Took to him right off, didn't you?' Wayne accused her. He thrust his way roughly through the undergrowth. 'Trenton is just the kind of guy no woman can ignore. He's got Leigh eating out of his hand like a little bird.'

A vulture, Sara thought but did not say. Tears filled her eyes as a branch Wayne released whipped back and hit her across the cheek. She sagged back to lean against a tree and as she did so, her back came in contact with a furry plant covered with stiff hairs.

'Oh my God!' The pain of the stings spread right through her body and she jerked away quickly staring at the dense undergrowth of shrubs and seedling trees around her.

'Sara, what is it?' Wayne who had been forging ahead, his mind preoccupied with resentments, trekked back to her.

'I've been stung.' She clutched her shoulder tightly. 'Obviously by that shrub.' She inclined her head towards a shrub with large insect-eaten leaves. 'Maybe the birds and the insects don't suffer any harm but I'm a mass of stings.'

'Where, on your back?'

'Oh, Wayne, don't touch me.'

'Your blouse is covered with sharp hairs,' he said in a concerned voice, hesitating as though he didn't know what to do next.

'Do me a favour. Turn away, I'm going to take it off.'

'Good idea,' Wayne encouraged her. 'Hang on, I'll get Leigh to help you.' He began to move away and Sara bit her lip in helpless exasperation. Wayne as a man couldn't be measured on the same scale as Wayne the artist.

'What's happened here?' It was Guy who returned and Sara hastily pulled the open front of her blouse together.

'For God's sake, don't get embarrassed,' he said shortly, 'You've been stung, haven't you?'

'You bet I have!' she said sarcastically. 'But don't you worry too much, I'll survive.'

'Let me see, Sara.' He reached out from his imposing height. 'You're wearing a bra, aren't you?'

'I started when I was about fourteen.'

'Your temper may yet destroy you.' His fingers very gently began to peel the blouse from her. 'Slip it off, there's a good girl. You must be in agony.'

'Hmmm.' It was showing very plainly in her pale face and enormous eyes.

Pain or not, she was shocked by the touch of his fingers on her bare skin. She was trembling but he held her with one hand and very skilfully removed the several hairs that had broken off and pierced her skin. 'That's a sorry-looking sight,' he said quietly. 'Your beautiful skin is inflamed. I'll tell you what we'll do: swallow a couple of pain-killers and perhaps an antihistamine and I'll scout around for the plant the aboriginals use as an antidote. It usually grows close by, but it's small. We'll boil it up and put the cooled liquid on your skin. It's said to work.'

'I hope so!' Sara dashed away the tears of pain angrily.

'You can't put that blouse on again. In fact it's so covered with hairs we might as well throw it away. The only good thing is it protected you from worse harm.' As he talked he was already stripping off his shirt. 'Here, put this around you until you can find something else.' He turned her to him, his brilliant eyes glittering. 'Don't look like that, little one.'

'How?' She lifted her head and her beautiful mouth quivered.

'So bloody vulnerable,' he said without preamble. 'I hate this to happen to you, Sara. I could have taken it myself.'

'My hero!' Her face lit with a wry smile.

'In the forest . . . yes. I dare say you'll be back to normal by the time I get you out.' He didn't smile, a faint whiteness beneath his polished bronze skin. 'You look very fragile in my shirt.'

'Thank you, Guy.' She looked down, deliberately veiling her eyes.

'My pleasure,' he said gently, his eyes on her glowing halo of hair. 'I'm quite sure you'd give me the shirt off your own back.'

The others were resting in a small group some fifty yards on and it was the two men, not Leigh, who sprang up.

'Wayne, get a couple of Panadol out of the first-aid kit and an antihistamine,' Guy directed. 'Leigh, do you think you can find another shirt for Sara? She dare not put the other one back on. It's covered in stinging hairs.'

'How is it, Sara?' Wayne knelt over the first-aid kit, while Jake walked a little unevenly towards her.

'Pretty painful.' In fact the pain was so severe she felt ill.

'You look ghastly,' Leigh supplied.

'Does ghastly mean her eyes are too big for her face?' Jake, who up until then had been quiet and almost deferential, turned on Leigh angrily. No one had mentioned it but it was painfully obvious Leigh had taken it into her head to be jealous of Sara.

Leigh for her part flushed deeply. 'What did she expect if she goes swinging through the jungle? Might I remind you there was a serpent even in Paradise.'

Angry though he was, Jake couldn't bring himself to utter what came to mind. He went to Sara and squeezed her hand. 'I seem to remember there's some kind of antidote for these stings, love.'

'That's right.' Guy removed the rifle from his arm. With his torso bare he looked incredibly fit and powerful and Leigh was staring at him so devouringly she seemed incapable of carrying on the search for another garment for Sara. 'I want you all to rest here for while and I'll go looking. I don't think it should take me long. These plants are said to grow almost side by side.'

'I'll come with you,' Jake immediately offered, but Guy turned to him quietly. 'Thanks, Jake, but I'll move faster on my own. You could boil up some water. We'll take a break and make up some lotion for Sara. She's playing hardy, but that must hurt like hell.'

Even then Sara had to cross back to Leigh and select a cream cotton shirt for herself. She picked it up and started towards a veil of ferns.

Guy came after her with his cat-like tread, pausing for a moment while she slipped his shirt off and the cream shirt on. 'Hang on in there, Sara,' he said abruptly, though some note in his voice brushed her like a shock. 'Your ordeal won't last any longer than I can help.'

That night they camped at the base of another rain-forest giant with its distinctive woody caves, and Sara's heart leapt in her throat as wave after wave of large bats shrieked overhead, fanning out to feed on the wealth of wild fruits. Progress had been delayed by her sharp bout of sickness, but the native lotion Guy had applied to her back had proved far more effective than she could have hoped for. She began to appreciate then the wealth of knowledge the aboriginals possessed about their native plants and their poisonous or curative properties. Although she still felt the stings, the almost unbearable pain had subsided to a mild smarting.

They dined on pigeon, even Leigh, and, exhausted by physical exertion, for they had come through undergrowth waist-deep, fell quickly into uneasy sleep. Jake had been quite lucid all day but was uncharacteristically low on energy. It was Guy's opinion he was in shock and his mind was giving him no peace. Though they had survived thus far, Jake seemed to be taking personal responsibility for the crash.

'Does it strike you, Sara, we could die here?' Wayne asked her, looking apprehensively around him. 'We're right off the map and we're following Guy blindly.'

'There's food and there's water.' Sara felt too weak to comfort him. 'We've elected Guy our leader and I'm not going to question him.'

'Who elected him?' Wayne moved his blanket closer to Sara. 'None of the rest of us got a chance.'

'I can understand why,' Sara sighed. 'Jake's far from well and deeply troubled. Leigh is nearly hysterical in this kind of situation. You said yourself you could never qualify as a bushman and I'm impressively trouble-prone. Even tree snakes drop on my shoulder.' She had, in fact, had that gruesome experience just before sunset, but Guy had removed the snake so swiftly her panic had just stopped short of overcoming her. Now she lived in dread of its happening again, despite Guy's assurances.

As she lay on her side, Wayne leaned over and kissed the corner of her mouth. 'Forgive me, Sara. You would never have found yourself in this terrible situation but for me.'

She reached up and patted his torn and bruised hand. 'It's not *all* bad, Wayne. I'm fascinated by the forest. It's incredibly beautiful, even if I could do without a few of the reptiles. In fact I'd be enjoying this immensely if we were on a recognised expedition and we were properly equipped.'

Wayne lay back with a horrified expression on his face. 'You're full of surprises, aren't you? It never occurred to me that a beautiful career-girl might hanker after primitive adventure.'

'So what about you?' Wearily Sara closed her eyes. 'You paint this tropical environment so brilliantly, yet you seem to prefer your imaginings to reality. From your exhibitions I would have thought you spent a lot of time meticulously studying the great wilderness on your doorstep.'

'One doesn't have to climb a rain-forest giant to paint an orchid. The entire north is rich in birdlife, brilliant flora, hot peacock skies. I prefer to paint in the open woodland. That's quite wild enough for me. The rain-forest canopy gives me claustrophobia. There are plenty of magnificent water-lily lagoons in the grasslands. If we ever get back to civilisation there are so many wonderful sights I can show you. Val will be sick with worry by now. What about your parents? They'll be frantic.'

'Yes,' Sara murmured bleakly. 'My father is apt to demand instant action. I would say there's a search on for us now.'

'Without a doubt.' Wayne's brown eyes were sunk in shadows. 'Trenton's disappearance will be big news. It will be all over the papers and on the TV, but finding the point to penetrate the jungle would be like trying to find a needle in a haystack.'

Guy urged them up at first light and Sara abruptly turned away as Leigh sobbed out her cramped and aching muscles cradled against his chest. Wayne, too, must have found the sight too bitter for his taste, because he kicked viciously at the put-out fire managing to cover a large lizard in ashes.

'Take it easy, Wayne.' Sara fanned off the ashes by swishing a small branch. 'Even if you're not engaged any more, I think you care about Leigh.'

'How can you say that, when she's shown what sort of person she is? I know it's been terrible, but she's never stopped moaning. She's been abominable to poor old Jake. As though it's his fault we were hit by bloody lightning! She hasn't shouldered one pack. She takes the lightest thing there is. *Her* cuts have to be attended to first. She hangs back and lets you prepare what food there is. She's one of the most selfish, pampered creatures alive.'

'I guess none of us falls in love to order.'

'I don't love Leigh, Sara.' Wayne slung a bag over his shoulder. 'My eyes were open to her long before I met you. You're beautiful and you're real. You have none of Leigh's unpleasant feline traits, none of her vanities. Her father made her the way she is. Her mother was a complete failure as a parent. She left it all to him, consequently Leigh grew up with a tremendous sense of self-importance—Daddy adores her and Daddy has all that money, Mummy is just a glorified slave.' He looked away quickly with an expression of angry defeat.

If I ever get out of here, Sara thought, I shan't want to be visiting Wayne. He was still in love with Leigh. That was it. No matter how clearly he perceived her limitations, he still wanted her, and Sara was not completely sure Leigh had overcome her feelings for Wayne. Maybe at the moment she had an overwhelming physical passion for Guy Trenton, but it was almost certainly unsatisfied. Guy had shown her no special treatment beyond being tolerant of her difficult moods. Sara suspected that when he did care about a woman his feelings would run very deep. She gave a deep sigh of resignation. Something in her yearned for such a man when every instinct warned her to run for her life.

'Leave that, Sara,' he ordered her as she picked up a pack.

'I can manage.'

'Be practical,' he told her quietly. 'The strap will cut into your shoulder and back. Take this, it's lighter.'

Sara took the overnight bag he passed her, but didn't reply.

Leigh, several feet away, must have taken it as some sort of a rebuff, because she smiled, her dark eyes sparkling maliciously in her thin, tanned face.

Mid-way through the long and difficult morning, Jake, without a sound, collapsed.

'Guy!' Sara cried out the alarm. He was well ahead, slashing strongly at the deep undergrowth.

'What now, for God's sake?' Leigh sank desperately to her knees, her once glossy hair lank with debris and sweat. 'Are we supposed to stay here while he recovers?'

'Why don't you consider other fears than yours?' Sara drew Jake's head up on to her breast. 'None of us are sure what's happening to Jake. He might be bleeding inside.'

'Sure he hasn't just collapsed?' Wayne drew closer, staring into the pilot's gaunt face. 'He's not so young, you know, and the going has been tough.'

'I'll have to make up that stretcher again,' Guy told them after a quick examination. 'He wants medical attention. His heart seems to be beating OK. I can't even guess.'

Now their progress was even slower because Guy had to scout the way before returning to help carry the stretcher.

'We'll never get out of here,' Leigh wailed.

'What a pity Daddy isn't here to help us!' Wayne bit off angrily, projecting his own hatreds. 'Instead of being so appallingly negative, why can't you be more like Sara?'

'Sara is having as much trouble standing up as I am!' Leigh yelled in a corresponding passion. 'Does she know what a coward *you* are? Does she know you lived off your mother until your weird paintings finally sold? Does she know you were going to kill yourself when you couldn't have me?'

'Any more, Leigh?' Guy growled at her in obvious disgust. 'Shouldn't private matters be kept to yourself?'

The contempt in his tone sobered her and they moved on.

The day wore on, the going so tough, Sara thought it might be very easy to die of thirst and exhaustion.

'I can't go any further, Guy,' Leigh gasped and began to crumple to the ground. 'We're doomed, I'm telling you.'

'*Rubbish!*' He wasn't reacting so tolerantly to her intermittent stream of protests and complaints. 'Has no one noticed that the character of the forest is changing?'

'Who the hell is an ecologist?' Wayne was finding it particularly difficult carrying the rear end of the stretcher when no such flagging in the bigger, more powerful Trenton could be observed.

'You must recognise the going has been getting easier over the last hour. Part of this is the changing nature of the forest, part of it because we're going down. The next stream we come to should be larger and faster-flowing, which isn't all that good for fish, but unlike yesterday the canopy of the forest isn't completely closed. That means we can be spotted more easily, even if we can't get ourselves completely out. It seems to me Jake could have suffered a mild heart-attack. It's been on my mind to leave you at camp and go on alone. I could move much faster and bring help.'

'No, Guy!' Leigh said very tightly. 'I wouldn't feel safe without you.'

'Thanks very much.' Colour stung in Wayne's brown faun-like face. 'Nor can I listen to your per-petual whining much longer. You've been croaking louder than the frogs.'

'Speaking of frogs,' Sara shook leaves and assorted birds' feathers out of her hair, 'does anyone fancy some for dinner? They've been too much of a deli-cacy for me up until now.'

Guy slanted a glance at her and laughed. 'Let's get going. Darkness falls quickly and we have to make a suitable camp.' He picked up his end of the stretcher again, gripped it tightly and, with his mouth com-pressed, Wayne did the same.

They were drenched by a late afternoon thunder-storm, but nobody, not even Leigh, complained. Wind and rain whipped overhead but nearly all of the tur-bulence was lost by the time the rain reached the forest floor. It cooled them off completely and ran like nectar into their open mouths. The birds loved it, shrieking their ecstasy high in the trees, but as suddenly as it had come on, the storm moved away and glorious beams of light shot through the treetops and illuminated small clearings with almost unearthly light. Everything was washed pure and the spectacular flowerings seemed to grow as one looked.

It came as an enormous shock when Guy suddenly put down the stretcher. He stood rigid, frozen like a jungle animal, and when Wayne demanded raggedly what was wrong he was told in no uncertain terms to shut up. Swiftly and very purposefully Guy slipped the strap of the rifle off his shoulder and began moving very slowly and stealthily towards a rustling in the leaves. It was growing louder and now they all heard it.

No matter what she had said, Leigh jumped towards Wayne for protection and he just as unthinkingly grasped her close. The light was getting poorer and they all strained their eyes to pierce the glistening undergrowth.

Jake lurched up, gripping Sara's shoulder, and using the last of his strength to force her roughly behind him. There was dread on his face and Sara felt an answering fear begin to squeeze the life out of her. Nevertheless she clutched at Jake's shirt and tried to urge him backwards. 'What is it? We don't have any tigers!'

Jake didn't answer but picked up a stout branch. Whatever it was, he feared it might do them harm.

When the boar charged it came with such speed against the green undergrowth it was a shiny black blur.

Leigh screamed and held tightly to Wayne's chest but Guy didn't fire until he was satisfied he could drop the wild boar with one shot. Head and shoulders were curved over the rifle while he stood motionless in striking contrast to the maddened charge of the heavily tusked and powerful animal.

Sara couldn't look any longer. She let her head fall against Jake's shoulder and squeezed her eyes shut. A boar's tusks had been known to disembowel a man, and just as she jerked up, Guy's single rifle shot found its way straight to the boar's brain.

'Hurray!' Jake yelled excitedly, but when he tried to rush to Guy's side he halted abruptly, hollowing his chest and clutching it with crossed arms.

'Jake!'

Sara's cry alerted Guy and he loped back quickly for an inspection of the fallen wild boar.

'It's OK. I'm OK. A bit of a chest pain, that's all. I've never had trouble with my ticker before.'

'Here, Jake, sit down.' Guy urged the older man into a semi-recumbent position. 'How's it now?'

'OK. It was just a stab.'

'Sure?'

'What a burden I've been to you,' Jake said.

'Listen, we're just so grateful you're around. That we're all around.' Sara stooped and kissed Jake on the cheek. 'Keep up your spirits, Jake. It will be so much better for you.'

Her kiss seemed to calm Jake down. 'I have been agonising about the whole thing,' he admitted reluctantly. 'I guess it doesn't help.'

'Don't talk. Quiet now for a while.' Guy gripped his shoulder, searching the pilot's face. 'When you feel easier, we'll go on. The boar would make a feast for an army.'

'Oh, yuck!' Leigh sagged, then collapsed into a dead faint.

CHAPTER FOUR

JUST as Guy predicted, they came on another mountain stream, much augmented by the run-off of storm water but unhappily short on fish.

'If this were plains country we might have had to share it with a crocodile,' Wayne told Sara wryly. 'I guess Trenton would have shot it and turned it into a nice stew. They reckon the tail tastes just like pork.'

'Well, it's pork tonight.' Sara felt the nerves and muscles of her stomach fluttering. 'How's Leigh? She won't let me go near her.'

'Because you show her up.' Wayne threw some sticks at a large hunting frog and slapped a shining, emerald beetle from his knee. 'This isn't Leigh's scene at all—mountain slopes and bubbling springs. She has never in her life had to rough it, much less survive a plane-crash. She feels trapped in a tortured environment. She doesn't know how to function when her body's not pampered and enclosed in silk. She acts so slick-tongued and ultra-confident but her nature's too fragile to withstand deprivation.'

'It's only been two days!' Sara was trying hard to understand. 'We've been adequately nourished. We have plenty of water. God, can you imagine what it might have been like if we crashed in the desert?'

'They might have found us sooner.'

'Probably, and very nicely baked. I'll take the jungle any day. It's rather terrifying, the size, but my spirit seems to be at peace in the wilderness. I must be lucky. Leigh only finds it fearful.'

'I'll make it up to you when we get out,' Wayne promised her, breathing in the fragrant scent that pervaded the air.

'Probably, Wayne, I'll have to go back home.'

'Don't say that!' Wayne turned to stare at her, marvelling that nothing, scratches, bruises, a total lack of make-up and torn and smeared clothing diminished her beauty. 'I want you quite *desperately* to stay. Everything that has happened to us has made me admire you more. You've tugged and tramped as good as a man.'

'I haven't,' Sara admitted wryly.

'Well, nearly as good.' Wayne put his arm around her waist, his eyes showing his ardency. 'You know I'm falling in love with you, don't you?'

'No, not really,' Sara responded a bit absentmindedly. Her real attention was on Guy's lean and powerful bent figure. He was checking on the amount of cooking of the roast pork. It was really her job, or it had been since the first day, but he had ordered her off to rest.

'You know I am!' Wayne gazed intently at her. 'It's quite extraordinary, here in the forest you're hauntingly beautiful. You even adorn your hair with tropical orchids and it's magnificent foaming away from your face and falling over your shoulders. Even your eyes are as green as the leaves.' He touched her cheek caressingly with his hand. 'I'd like to be the big jungle hero for you like Trenton's been for the past days, but you know that's not my style. I guess his height and strength predisposes him to play the hero. Honest to God, he's as strong as an ox, isn't he?'

Sara was unexpectedly goaded by the comparison. 'He's much too brilliant a creature to be likened to an ox. I'd have said more like a leopard or a lion. I never imagined anyone could have burnished eyes. Indeed they shine in the dark.'

'Perhaps you're falling in love with him?' Wayne made an overwhelming attack on a lime-green beetle.

'No, thank you.'

'Why not?' To her surprise he took her chin in his fingers and turned her face towards him. 'Just now you got fired up.'

'Surely not.' She had to struggle to convince him. 'Actually I'm a little afraid of Guy. There's such an air about him—such tremendous *male* endowment. I like to believe men and women are equal, but then along comes someone like Guy and even *I* can't believe it. He's so bold and brave and resourceful. He'd have made a good medieval king. Men like that give women a hard time. I suppose I have a complex about men who have too much natural and hence acquired power. It's difficult for them *not* to behave in an absolute, autocratic fashion. I grew up in a household where my father dominated every aspect of our lives. While my mother and I appeared to have everything in this world, a lovely home, plenty of money to buy clothes, since our looking good enhanced my father, the fact is, we both learned we had to bend to his will to enable us to live in peace. Why am I a journalist? Because my father barred me from studying law. If I hadn't given up for my mother's sake, I think he would have arranged that I didn't make the quota. He wanted no other lawyers in the family, much less a woman QC.'

'But wouldn't it be a stressful profession?' Wayne asked her kindly. 'Probably you wanted to be a lawyer for the very reason your father didn't want you to be. You *do* have a spirited nature.'

'That was suggested to me too, Wayne.' Sara leaned back against the boulder. 'Men seem to translate a woman's opposite wishes into defiance. I really wanted to study law with a view to helping my own sex with the legal processes. I've seen and heard of a lot of injustice. Women can be very easily manipulated and their vulnerability is well known. I earned my place on the Evan Kirkman Show with one particular interview I did on a harassment case. The man was an important and influential businessman. Too many people tried to write the young girl off as "provocative" mostly because she was very pretty. My interview showed rather clearly how innocent she was of any provocative tactics. It was my interview that got her version coverage.'

'You have a considerable social conscience.'

'Hey now, that sounded like it bothered you.'

'Don't be silly,' Wayne said quietly, 'but you take too much out of yourself.'

'I suppose I have been simmering all these years,' Sara shrugged. 'Oppression tends to make the natives fierce.'

'Hey, that smells good!' Wayne looked towards the fire in surprise. 'No reason why it shouldn't taste good either.'

'I suppose I should have another go at talking to Leigh,' Sara sighed. 'She's all huddled up there, looking very miserable. She decided not to take a dip after all, the water was so cold.'

'No need to bother her.' Wayne stroked his unshaven face. 'I was wondering what she is to Trenton. *She* seems mesmerised to me, but *he* doesn't appear particularly interested.'

'It's not exactly the time nor the place,' Sara pointed out wryly. 'There's a bit too much discomfort to feel romantic.'

'Then how come his eyes flash when he looks at you?'

Sara swung her head in surprised disbelief. 'That's a bit of an exaggeration, isn't it?'

'He's not one half as interested in Leigh as he is in you.'

'Don't you think that's because I'm standing up to this a bit better?'

'My dear,' Wayne pointed out rather bitterly, 'when you suffer, *he* suffers. He found Leigh's dead faint a bit of a bore but when you backed into that stinging tree it really tore him up.'

'Well, I did suffer for a while.' Sara looked very doubtful. 'Guy's the sort of man who saves the women and children first.'

'And I'm not?' Wayne's light, attractive voice was very flat.

'It's just an expression.' Sara began to feel uneasy. Surely Leigh's little jealousies were enough?

'You haven't forgotten I had to leave you when we were all running away from the plane.'

'Wayne, I understand!' Sara swiped at a flying insect that emerged from her hair. 'When a plane is about to explode I have no quarrel with each man for himself. Besides, your first concern was for Leigh. Do you realise that?'

'I only know I feel guilty about leaving *you*. I'd be happy to have the moment over again and I'd stay. It's curious when one thinks one is about to die. The first thought is just to run. If Leigh and I were running together it's simply because we were the first to hit the ground.'

'Don't go over it, Wayne,' Sara advised. 'There would have been no advantage returning for me if we'd all blown up. I blame you for nothing. Please believe it.'

'If I had a drink I'd get drunk,' Wayne muttered intensely. 'You know now, Sara, I don't react all that well in a crisis. Trenton renounced his chance at life to help Jake and you. His precise moment came to make a choice and it didn't take him a second. I guess it's a sense of honour, valour, whatever. Men like Trenton are capable of that. For that matter, *you* stayed. Leigh's only thought was to head off.'

'It makes sense, Wayne. Forget it. Given the nature of the circumstances no one in this world would blame you for not getting stuck beneath a plane that could have exploded at any minute. You're hungry, tired. It's enough to depress anyone.'

To get right away from the subject, Sara stood up and walked back to where Leigh was huddled. 'How are you feeling now, Leigh?' she asked quietly.

'I've decided I don't want any dinner.'

'You should eat, don't you think? I'll bring you a very small portion and I'll cut it very thin.'

'Don't bother,' Leigh shuddered. 'I would only throw it up.'

'Such a pity there doesn't seem to be any fish. Guy said the water was too fast-flowing.'

'Wayne been sobbing in your ear?' Leigh asked shortly.

'About what?' Sara lowered herself slowly to the older girl's side.

'Wayne's a man with many fears.'

'Artists are usually rather complicated,' Sara said mildly, trying to avoid a bitter discussion. 'He's gaining quite a reputation in the art world. Do you know that?'

'Sure.' Leigh laughed. 'That's the only thing he things about, his work. You'd think he was Gauguin or Van Gogh. One of the greats!'

'Well, he mightn't be in that category—few are—but he's very gifted. He has a big future. His big canvases command quite a few thousand these days.'

'He painted me, did you know? I look terribly neurotic and disturbed, though opinions differ. Daddy thought it so terrible it put him in quite a rage but my mother thought it an excellent likeness. It's difficult to explain. Some think it marvellous but Daddy and I think it rather "destructive". Anyway I kept it. It's worth money, hence acceptable. Oh, yes, Wayne ensnared me for a time. He's such an insinuating creature. One feels almost protective of him as a mother does of a child. Not that he doesn't have a subtle sexual attraction. Nothing like Guy, of course.

He's positively radiant. I don't think I've ever seen or felt such sexual energy. He incorporates *everything* a woman thinks of as splendidly male. Wayne, on the other hand, has no great masculine qualities. You've seen his reactions since we crashed. He's given a rather poor account of himself, even if Guy has tried to cover up his inadequacies. I hate it that he's so weak. Of course his stupid mother has protected him all his life. She raised him to believe he was a boy genius even when his father tried to interest him in the land. His childhood wasn't normal. His mother adores him and she's not prepared to renounce him unless it's to a woman like herself. Someone who is going to devote her whole life to looking after Wayne Palmer, the great artist. Someone who will feed him when he neglects to eat. Change his clothes.'

'Do you still love him, Leigh?' Sara asked very softly.

Leigh reacted as though stabbed. 'Of course I don't. How could I love a man I don't respect? Daddy sorted him out right off and he was pretty blunt about it. My father is a realist. He's also a very secure and successful man. Small wonder he had no time for Wayne, the drifter.'

'Except he has finally established himself,' Sara pointed out a little coolly. 'Your father may not have seen Wayne's recent showings or read what the critics have to say, but surely he's heard some word?'

'There's been some talk since he returned. Strangely enough from Guy. But then Guy is a very cultured man. He considers artists far more valuable human beings than Daddy does. The big plantation house is full of paintings, sculptures, rugs, furniture, you name it. The Trentons have always lived like princes. The papers will have mounted a full coverage of his disappearance now. Since he finally settled here, after his father died, he's gone from strength to strength. Everything he touches turns to gold. Daddy thinks there's no better man in the entire north—make that the whole country.'

'And what do you think?' Sara turned to look into the other girl's strained and pale face.

'I think I'm in love with him.'

'Like a fantasy?'

'Like for real!' Leigh returned shortly. 'I'm twenty-six years old and I'm starting to get worried I'll never find a man to measure up.'

'To your father?'

'Don't start spouting any psychology,' Leigh advised her. 'There's nothing unusual about my admiration for my father. At the same time it makes it difficult for me to accept a lesser man. News of the crash must have been a terrible blow for Daddy.'

'Surely no less a blow for your mother?'

'My mother and I have been a little estranged for some time. But yes, she'll be tremendously upset. I'm an only child.'

They were still talking when Guy walked away from the fire to join them. 'I've taken great trouble with this. I hope you're going to be able to eat a few mouthfuls, Leigh.'

'I'll try,' she said almost shyly.

'You need building up. You're a feather-weight.'

In fact the roasted flesh of the boar was a little tough but quite palatable, even without the sprinkling of salt Sara usually found indispensable. Jake ate little but Guy insisted he didn't lie down before he had time to digest the small portion of white meat. He had experienced no further pain but it was evident Guy was taking no chances.

Above the thinned canopy of the forest the stars were brilliantly shining and there was the constant flutter of bats' wings against the soft purple sky. The trees were alive with possums ripping and tearing the leaves and fruits that made up their exclusively vegetable diet, and Guy carried a flaming brand in his hand so that Sara could see a whole group quietly munching on some yellow-green fruit. Their eyes shone brilliantly, reflecting the light, then a second later they scurried off, the females in the group carrying their joeys in the pouch or on their backs.

Afterwards Sara walked down to the pool to splash her face with the cold water, then to sit on an overhanging rock and dangle her feet in the water. The pool was much larger than the other one with the twin waterfalls, and the water was moving faster. From the branches overhanging the water, tree frogs sat like Buddhas waiting for flying insects to offer themselves to their flicking tongues, or the male frogs called in an effort to attract a mate. It was so quiet, Sara could hear the leaves fall and the more adventurous frogs fording the fast-running stream and landing with a 'plomp' on some rock. Strange little orchids grew at the base of the rocks, green with a hood. She did not see the snake that swam with sinuous motion across the crystal pool. It was harmless in any case, although the taipan, the most dangerous snake on the continent, hunted this territory.

For the survivor of a crash, she felt curiously at peace.

Guy, who had been observing her for some minutes, left his place at Jake's side to join her. Jake was quietly drowsing and Leigh and Wayne were having one of their short but frequent heated discussions. It seemed almost impossible for Leigh to retain the insults she had hoarded up, just as it seemed impossible for Wayne not to go out of his way to elicit them.

'What are your plans for tomorrow, Guy?' Sara asked him.

'I'd like to go on ahead. I think it's our only hope to get help for Jake quickly. The rest of us can survive.'

'You'd better not tell Leigh. She doesn't have a great deal of confidence in the rest of us.'

'How do *you* feel, Sara? Would you be frightened?'

'Yes, probably.' Right at that moment she thought she couldn't bear it. 'How much longer do you think it would take?'

'Once I get to the edge of the rain-forest I'll be spotted in the open woodland. The authorities will be searching for us.'

'Isn't the edge of the rain-forest ferocious to break through? I think I read once it's like a solid wall of thorn-studded vines. What if anything happened to you? What if you trod on a venomous snake? It would be as bad worrying if you didn't make it as . . .'

'As what?'

'Go if you have to go, Guy,' she sighed quietly. 'I think you're right. Jake is having a bit of trouble with his heart. The concussion we worried about seems to have passed. Who knows what's really going on? He could have had a mild attack when he collapsed.'

'It's a pity Wayne isn't more of a bushman,' he said finally. 'I guess a man can't be everything.'

'You're not doing too badly.'

'From aggression to a little admiration? My image *has* improved.' He gave a brief, amused laugh.

'That's the paradox of the war between the sexes.'

'And why would you feel you *must* be pitted against me? Is it pre-ordained or something?'

'Why not?' She looked at him through heavy lashes. 'You're the archetypal male and I'm a rampaging feminist!'

'You can be a bit sharp when you want to be,' he agreed.

'I'm serious,' she said wistfully.

'I know, and I appreciate your dedication, but don't let it become a preoccupation in your life. There are masses of men out there on your side. I'd even cite myself, but to no avail. You've decided, on the basis of the way I look, that you know what I'm all about. Of course it's anger without an outlet, but all the same it's not fair, Sara, and I've found you to be very brave and generous.'

'You're the one taking care of us.'

'Tell me what's in your secret heart. I swear I'll listen.'

She shook her head. 'Not here. Not now.'

'How would you like to stay at my plantation house? It's filled with things I'm sure you'd love.'

'You're really sure you're going to get us out?'

'Aren't you?' He tilted his bold dark head to the side.

'You're the most extraordinary man I've ever met.'

'So why are you afraid of me?' There was little apology for his blunt and vaguely dangerous tone.

'Trauma. Fixed traumas.' She made a little wry face.

He took her hand and turned it up, pressing his thumb into her palm. 'Why were you running away from Kirkman? Had he become a problem?'

'No, *no*!' In fact she was reacting to the deep stirrings within her; the friction of his skin against hers.

'You'll have to do better than that, Sara. I monitored every one of your expressions at the airport.'

'Why?' She tried to withdraw her hand but couldn't. 'You don't seem such a *curious* person.'

'Except you riveted my attention just as I riveted yours. You know that.'

'I know nothing of the kind. Don't do that,' she pleaded.

'All right.' He turned her hand over but still held it lightly. 'Why does danger, isolation, heighten every one of our senses? It would be so damnably easy to make love to you.'

'Because you have every woman you want?'

'There are a lot I leave alone, so take that look off your face. I'm no womaniser.'

'Yet you radiate sexual power.'

'Lucky me!' He shrugged as though it was something he didn't care about. 'In any case, you must have discovered that about yourself.'

'Fighting off seduction is a familiar condition.'

'You think having your portrait painted is a better ploy?'

'Wayne is a friend.'

'All the more reason to consider before embarking on an affair. Wayne needs a woman to depend on. A woman who might closely resemble his mother. Oh, not in looks, but a woman who sees service as her destiny. Wayne as an artist must be free to abandon himself to his work, which means the woman in his life would have to apply herself even more diligently to the housework. A compliant nature would be crucial, I'm sure.'

'Are you saying I don't have one?'

'Surely you've been asserting yourself all your life? You reacted so violently to *me*, one could assume you've been alienated from what you call "the archetypal male" for some considerable time. This could explain in turn your preference for boyish men like Kirkman and Palmer. The more adult variety put you in a panic.'

'Rubbish!'

'You have some pretty clear-cut images in your mind. Images that might be difficult to break down.'

'Go on. This amateur psychology is relatively harmless.'

'You are aware of the complexity of your feelings?'

'God knows I am while you're holding my hand.'

He laughed. 'I'd like to be kissing you at the very least. Be angry with me, Sara, but I adore red hair and green eyes.'

'Don't you like dark hair and dark eyes at all?'

'Ah. Leigh.'

'Didn't she come to meet you like a good friend?'

'And in doing so put herself though a lot of bad times.' He turned his head slightly so that he could sweep a glance over the camp. 'You didn't give her any more of those Valiums, did you? She seems drugged out.'

'It's tiredness. She's physically exhausted. She could have had another one, I suppose.'

'You don't need anything to calm you down?'

'I like to have my wits about me at all times.'

'They seem to be asleep with their heads together.'

'There's a lot of left-over emotion there, no doubt. I gather Leigh's father didn't like or approve of Wayne.'

'She told you?' He gave her an appraising look.

'He sounds like a proper bastard.'

'He is.'

Sara nodded. 'He convinced Leigh Wayne was a failure when he's practically guaranteed a sell-out these days.'

'Sutton knows nothing about art.'

'I believe you have a very beautiful home.' She took a deep breath and turned to look at him.

'Naturally there's plenty of room for guests.'

'You know I was invited to stay with Wayne and his mother.'

'What happens when you hit a rough patch?'

'What do you mean?'

His eyes seemed to shine like a cat's. 'It's all very well this talk about good pals, Sara, but for all your feminist views you still don't know the first thing about men. Put it another way; what happens when Wayne wants to make love to you?'

'I think I can manage that.'

He looked away. 'It might prove embarrassing. Val will take one look at you, the character and strength beneath the glamour-girl dazzle, and decide you're just the woman to take over her mantle. She's already your great admirer the way you dealt with him on the TV.'

'What would *you* know? You didn't see it.'

'I did. I have to relax like everybody else. I never expected Kirkman's show to be one half so good. You're one hell of an interviewer. You sliced through all that waffling in the sweetest, most engaging way. You reached out and turned what might have been a tense and academic performance into a litany of love. It was an excellent interview, but it was *your* magnetism that carried the day. You supplied the flash. Without you Wayne would have been articulate but dull.'

'Well, it's all over now,' she sighed. 'I quit my job.'

'Either that or become Kirkman's mistress?'

'He did offer to divorce his wife,' Sara said caustically. 'It made no difference at all to tell him I felt nothing. What man believes that? Career-women face a lot of problems, but I guess only a woman would understand a woman's problems. I didn't fancy sleeping with the boss to advance my career. So—no career. Or no future with that particular show.'

'I believe Lew Hardwick owns the channel.'

'So?'

'I know Lew, and he's the kind of man who would be unwilling to allow that kind of thing to go on.'

'I don't want you to get to Sir Lewis. I could just imagine what Evan would say in return. A good-looking woman is stuck with the image of seductress. It goes without saying I would have provoked Evan. He would have found it reasonable to assume I was interested in him.'

'And you weren't?'

'No.' She felt her whole body stiffen.

'So what do you do next? Try to find an opening on another show, another channel?'

'I'd like to finish my book first. I have a little money.'

'What's it about?' He lifted a forefinger and tucked the mass of curls that were obscuring her profile behind her ear.

'Life. I guess it's partly autobiographical.'

'Connected with your childhood?'

'Are you done psychoanalysing me?'

'You can't expect that at this stage of our acquaintance!' He gave her a quick smile. 'You're a curious mixture, Sara. So bright and confident, yet so conscious of oppression. Your parents, friends, even Kirkman by the sound of him must be frantic with worry for you.'

'It is a terrifying thing, a plane-crash. No one will really know if we're dead or alive.'

'We were incredibly lucky,' he said after a time. 'Now I've got to do everything possible to get Jake out tomorrow. He needs medical attention. A couple of days can be a very long time when something serious is going on. I wish to God I had a chain-saw. The machete's not much help to me any more.'

Looking at him, staggeringly strong and handsome, Sara felt a frightening pull of desire. It was so powerful she thought some of it had to show on her face. She started up so violently she slipped and he bent over and scooped her up.

'Put me down, Guy,' she said carefully.

'Surely it's better than the old days, with a wallop on the head?'

'You do have a primitive streak.'

'You bet I do,' he bit off bluntly. 'Thank your lucky stars the refining process was almost through.'

Hours later, Sara jerked up from her rug, her heart pounding in fear. Surely someone, something, some *form*, had been standing motionless staring at her from the glimmering shelter of the trees? She was sure she had been awake, eyes open, though now her gaze was swimming, curiously unfocused. She blinked violently, three or four times, staring with intensity across the orange glow of the fire to the ring of rain-forest trees.

Of course there was the possibility that she had been dreaming, but she could practically swear she had seen something with her conscious mind. From high in the trees came the sound of the legions of possums cracking and gnawing on nuts and decaying wood with their strong teeth. There was no breeze but the huge frond of a tree fern moved, then a soft, persistent sawing noise. The forest was alive with nocturnal animals but her vision, hallucination, had taken the outline of a man.

She dashed up unthinkingly and almost scuttled to where Guy Trenton was lying, his jet-black head turned on to his arm.

'Guy!' she whispered sharply, grasping his sleeve and shaking his arm.

He came awake instantly, not rolling or moaning or peering dimly to see who it was but as quick and ferocious as a jungle cat under attack.

One moment Sara was crouched over him, the next flat on her back, incapable of movement or voice. Her arms were pinned above her head and he was leaning over her, a muscle beside his mouth working.

'God, Sara!'

All she could manage was a soft little gasp.

'Sara!' He put his arm beneath her and lifted her. 'Hell, did you have to pick such a time?'

'You murderous maniac! You could have killed me.' She tried to detach herself from his arms but she couldn't.

'I'm sorry. So sorry.' He held her head back by the hair staring into her pearly face. 'I don't suppose you know what it's like being in places of danger. I reacted instinctively, I'm afraid.'

'I'll try to remember never to do it again.'

'Have I hurt you?' He ran his hand down the slope of her shoulder to her wrist.

'You've nearly knocked the breath out of me.'

'God!' he sighed, an unmistakable look of concern on his bold face. 'Oddly enough I'd been dreaming about you. We were in the middle of an argument. *You* were in the middle of an argument. You're the fire-brand.'

'I thought someone was staring at me.'

'What?' His voice was rather dry.

'I am absolutely serious.'

'Oh, absolutely.' He bent his head unexpectedly and buried it in her curling mass of hair.

'Guy.' She jerked her head back.

'I still don't understand why you've come to me,' he said wryly, 'you're obviously full of fight.'

'It's simple really,' she hissed. 'I saw someone, something, and I'm positive I wasn't dreaming.'

'How big was this something?' His topaz eyes sparkled.

'It looked pretty much like a man.'

'Yes, I suppose.' He looked about swiftly. 'Sure it wasn't Wayne?'

'Wayne's snoring.' In fact a muffled snore did float through the air. 'Perhaps you would care to search.'

He grasped her firmly under the arms and lifted them both to their feet. 'It could have been a wallaby.'

'I dare say,' she said edgily.

'There's nothing to alarm you, Sara.' His arm curled around her waist. 'Wait here. I'll take a look about.'

'What about the rifle?'

He laughed beneath his breath. 'Haven't you heard about my black belt?'

He worked his way around the camp in a circle, losing himself to Sara's eyes so that she drew a quick breath of relief when his tall powerful figure was thrown up by the leaping flames.

'Nothing,' he said.

'So why are you frowning?'

He shrugged. 'Whatever it was, it's gone.'

'I'm sorry,' she said abruptly. 'You get so little rest.'

'Stay with me.'

'What?' Her heart gave a painful lurch.

He turned and picked up her rug, throwing it on the ground so that it touched his spread jacket.

'Come here.'

'Guy?' She moved in a kind of agitation and he moved forward and grasped her hand.

'My darling girl, if you've any idea of seducing me, forget it.'

'I certainly haven't!'

'Then lie down. I'm dead tired.'

She felt a queer lack of resistance. She just lay on her side with her head turned away from him.

'How are you?'

'Fine. Just fine.'

'Say goodnight, Guy.'

'Goodnight, Guy.'

'How did it ever come to pass that you and I share a rug?'

'All I want is to get out of here.' All at once her whole body trembled.

'Sara, what is it?' He touched her shoulder.

'Nothing. I'll be all right.'

'You know there's nothing out there. Nothing to hurt you.'

It made no sense at all, but she felt like crying. She was quite startled in fact when a tear slid down her cheek.

'Sara, little one, I've never seen you helpless.' He turned her so that she lay on her back.

'It's this place. Nothing but the birds and trees and all the little animals in the jungle.'

'They don't threaten you.'

'No.' Her breath was a fluttering sigh.

'It's late. Go to sleep.' His voice was a mixture of teasing and tension.

'I will if you'll allow me to.'

He brushed the tear from her cheek with exquisite tenderness. 'Why did you break with Kirkman?'

'What a crazy question!' Rigid, she half lifted herself up.

'Did you love him at one time?'

'God, I hate *you*!'

'You have to. For a beautiful, highly intelligent girl you're not at all secure.'

'Don't you think this is a strange time to start a conversation?'

'Yes, I do, but why leave it? Why did you fall in love with Kirkman?'

'Were you there?' she asked him.

'Just answer me.'

'I wasn't even remotely in love with him. In fact I found all his posturing incredibly boring. I guess he wanted me because I represented a challenge.'

'There's a kind of resemblance between Kirkman and Palmer.'

'I'm not in love with Wayne either.'

'Then your behaviour seems so...odd. Do you want *me* to make love to you?'

'Here?' She felt a jut of excitement she disguised in an angry gasp.

'No, not here. I can pick you up. Carry you where no one could ever find us.'

She felt his hand in her hair, the brush of his skin against her cheek. 'What's your game, Trenton?'

He laughed, the tips of his fingers stroking her white temple and along her cheekbone. 'I've always liked puzzles.'

She stared up into the darkness, the effort to stop trembling unbearable. No matter how he caused it she had never felt such sexual excitement in her life. She had been kissed many times, yet she had never experienced more sensation than what was there in his fingertips. They continued down her small, straight nose and around the full curves of her mouth.

'Aaah!' he murmured as she bit at his finger. 'How many times *have* you been made love to?'

'That's certainly none of your business.'

'I'm merely asking.'

As he was, she was barely whispering. It was extraordinarily intimate. 'Hundreds of times. Does that shatter you?'

'It would if you were telling the truth.'

'Remarkable, isn't it? A man is free to have all the affairs he likes but a woman has to keep herself for the man who wishes to enslave her for life.'

'You have no great respect for men?' His fingertips stopped their stroking as he stared into her eyes.

'Why should I?' She heaved a deep and anguished sigh.

'Poor Sara! Didn't I tell you one sweet night we'd talk about how you were raised. I have a feeling that's when it started.'

'I've told you enough.'

'Mm, for the moment.' He bent his head and lightly brushed her mouth. It was electrifying, and Sara felt a little moan flit through her parted lips.

He drew back abruptly as though he were trying to keep himself in check, but then she gave another muffled sob and his strongly muscled arm slipped beneath her.

'*Sara!*' It was a groan from deep inside him.

'No, I *can't.*'

'Nothing is going to happen. I can only kiss you.'

'I know.'

'So let me taste your mouth.'

She surrendered all control that was left to her, alight with such yearning she arched her back upwards, locking her slender arms behind his dark head.

'One day I'll get you in bed.' He crushed her body to him, his kiss so deliriously deep and savage it bruised her full cushiony mouth.

Her fingers buried themselves in his thick hair, her mind engulfed, her flesh a medium for torrent upon torrent of insinuating sensation. She had known and wanted this all along. Antagonism was only part of it. A small part at the corner of her brain. Her body craved his, his magnetism enveloping her and drawing her in.

She gasped aloud, then almost stopped breathing when his hand sought her high, rounded breast, his fingers hard and callused curving over the soft, creamy slope, determined on the tightly peaked bud. When his fingers gently twisted the nipple her whole body jumped and a trail of fire shot from her breast to her core.

'Guy!' Her heart was thundering in her breast, her legs writhing, her need for him so appalling it was little different from grief.

'Come here to me!' As he bent his lips to her breast she twisted away violently, as though in the greatest danger, the scent of him filling her nostrils, her mouth and the dark, velvety air. She was doubled up as if in pain.

'Woman, what's *wrong* with you?' His voice had a peculiar tone, not tight nor thwarted, but desperate to know more.

'I'm sorry... I'm sorry.'

He flipped her back so that he was leaning atop of her. 'Hush now!' He cupped his hand around her neck and let it stay there.

'It's the only way I know to defend myself.'

'From me?' He soothed her shudders.

'So you terrify me!'

'How could *I* hurt you, Sara?' He looked down into her sensitive, tormented face.

'More than you know.'

There were tears at the corners of her eyes and he bent his head and licked them up with his tongue. 'What if I told you I would never allow it to happen?'

'What chance would I have against you?' she said in a pleading whisper. 'You're everything that draws me and everything I don't need.'

'I sense your problems, Sara.' He stroked the curling mass of her hair away from her heated face.

'And they've scarred me, don't you see that?'

'They've *scared* you,' he murmured steadily. 'There's a big difference between those two points. You have to come to terms with your prejudices, Sara. You can't blame all men because one hurt you very badly. What kind of man is your "safe" man anyway? Palmer? Kirkman because he was married? Don't you see your prejudices could cause you to make false judgements?'

She turned her face aside. 'Either way I'd never be able to deal with you, even if you wanted me, which of course you don't. The shocks of the last days have simply overtaken us. We've been forced into such close physical contact. Now we're exploiting it.'

'Really?' His voice was very dry. 'You don't believe that?'

'Then how do you explain it?'

'I certainly won't reduce it to a mindless sex drive. I see *you*, the whole woman, Sara, not some radiant vehicle on which to vent my sexuality. I've known quite a few beautiful women in my life without being in the least tempted to make love to them. I should add most of the time I've been given the green light. But desire for me is a total thing: mental, spiritual, physical. Would you be as drawn to me if my *mind* weren't the same? I'm as real to you as you are to me. The sooner you see that the better.'

'So now you talk to me like a schoolgirl.' Her brilliant eyes flashed.

'I'm only trying to set you straight. Now, which side of the rug do you prefer to sleep on?'

The kindness and mockery in his voice hurt her. 'Go to hell!'

'Mild-tempered redheads are rare.' He got his hand under her hips and arranged her comfortably. 'You're a very interesting case, Sara. You can hardly expect me to give up on you.'

CHAPTER FIVE

SARA awoke the next morning with the hair standing up on the back of her neck. A slight young man was crouching down near the fire and as she gave an involuntary little gasp he looked her way and gave her a reassuring grin.

'Mornin', miss!'

Sara found herself nodding. He didn't seem the kind to make trouble. He was aboriginal, his skin milk chocolate, his eyes liquid black, his curly hair shiny black. He was wearing cowboy garb and he looked wary but in no way frightened.

She rose quickly and went down to him. 'You were around the camp last night, weren't you?'

Before he could reply Guy's voice cracked out. 'Sara!' He came into sight, the rifle slung over his shoulder.

The boy—he couldn't have been more than seventeen—swung his head. 'Not doin' nuthin', boss.'

Leigh was up, making a sudden angry sweep towards them. 'What the devil is going on. Who is he?' Behind her Jake was straining up and Wayne was rising to his feet, face and body tense.

'Where did you come from?' Guy asked the boy firmly.

'Watch him, Guy!' Leigh shouted.

The boy lifted his arms away from his skinny frame. 'I got nuthin', boss. Wouldn't hurt no one anyway.'

'I realise that,' Guy said more mildly. 'You're from a station?'

The boy hung his head uncomfortably. 'Goon-gulba. Got into a bit of trouble.'

'So you took off for the rain-forest?' Sara asked incredulously. 'Surely there are better places to be?'

'None better for me, missy. The spirits talk to me. I don't feel frightened.'

'You're hungry?'

'A little. Ain't had much for a time.'

'You'll get some when you tell us what kind of trouble you're in,' Guy told him.

'Perhaps he killed someone,' Leigh supplied dramatically.

The boy laughed. 'I ain't killed no one, boss. I jes' fall in love.'

A feeling of intense relief swept over Sara. 'And she belonged to someone else. Someone older?'

The boy nodded and sighed. 'Old Creeper. He don't need her like we need each other.'

'Let's not bother with that for a moment.' Guy ran his hand over his darkened jaw. 'How long have you been in the forest? How many days?'

'Been gone a week. I push on.'

'How far is the station?'

The boy appeared not to have heard the question. 'Funny,' he scratched his head and looked around the camp in wonderment, 'what you doin' here? White people don't come here. Not so far.'

'Our plane crashed in the jungle,' Guy explained. 'Miles from here. You can understand what I'm saying? One of our party needs medical attention. How far is the property?'

'Take yah two days.' He looked at Guy consideringly. 'All of yah. Take *you* one, I reckon.'

'What about you?' Guy countered. 'I've never met an aboriginal who wasn't a first-class tracker.'

'I can't go back, boss,' the boy shrugged. 'Old Creeper would wring my neck.'

'Don't you worry about that. I'll straighten things out. How long have you been following us?'

'You mean to say he's only shown himself now?' Wayne asked furiously, clutching his shirt together.

'Never seen yah fire until last night. I watched for a minute then went back to me hiding-place. Don't mean no trouble. I jes' wanted to talk to somebody.'

'Other than the spirits, you mean?' Guy laughed. 'You don't want to stay in the forest, do you? What about your girl?'

'Yeah, I know, I worry. But gotta hide out for a time.'

'From your own people, from Old Creeper?'

'Sure,' the boy agreed almost merrily. 'Said he'd chop me head off and feed it to the crows.'

'He was only trying to frighten you, of course,' Sara suggested uneasily. 'What about the station boss?'

'Oh, the boss don't mind. It's between me and Creeper. And he's old. Maybe forty.'

'Goodness!' Leigh gave a great shudder. 'Do you think this love-struck idiot could get us out?'

'I'm sure he would want to try.' Guy held the boy's eyes.

Jake sagged back against a tree and Sara dashed to his side.

'Are you OK, Jake?'

'Sure I am!' Jake tried to rally. 'Mr Trenton can move ahead with the boy. We're already on the right track. A helicopter could winch us up.'

'How can you trust him?' Leigh's dark eyes flashed scornfully.

'Well, I do,' Guy responded shortly. 'He knows what kind of trouble we're in. He won't be going back to Goongulba alone. I'm with him and I'm positive we'll be able to work things out.'

The boy looked Guy's tall, impressive frame up and down and that appeared to settle it. 'If I could jes— eat somethin', boss, to keep up my strength?'

*   *   *

By nightfall of the same day Sara felt sapped of all goodwill. She avoided Leigh altogether and spent much of her time exploring the pool, always with the camp in sight. She even managed to swim naked and wash her hair, but when she doubled back Wayne and Leigh were still slogging it out. Jake lay quietly with his eyes closed and every time Sara checked on him he smiled at her. Rescue was inevitable, and the copious flow of insults bounced harmlessly off him.

There was roast fowl for dinner and all of them sat drinking several cups of tea with plenty of sugar. It seemed to compensate for their restricted diet.

'Of course there will be an investigation.' Leigh couldn't seem to leave the subject alone.

'Not much of one, I should think.' Sara inspected her mug carefully. 'Guy might try to push on during the night.'

'Have you any idea what we would have done without him?' Leigh, bone-thin, slipped a cabin pillow behind her back. 'The will to survive, to *succeed* is so strong in him.'

Wayne followed Sara down to the stream while she washed out their few utensils. 'Jake seems a bit improved.'

'Relief, I guess. With any luck at all we might be out of here by tomorrow afternoon.'

'You've been splendid, Sara.' Wayne sat back on a moss-covered boulder. 'You get to know people pretty fast under these conditions.'

'It does help a bit.' Sara started to look around for twigs for the fire.

'Sit down for a moment, can't you? You've had plenty of time for Trenton.'

'Don't start that again, Wayne.' Sara looked into the mirror-like pool of water. A copper moon was beaming down on them, a few clouds across it like a devil's mask. The beautiful voice of a nightbird was calling, then another, its mate.

'I'm sorry. Trenton's unmistakably hero material, while I'm low on such qualities.'

'I think Leigh has made you feel wretched. You've coped like the rest of us.'

'I've never known her in such evil moods.'

'Lack of food, do you think?' Sara suggested. 'She's barely touched anything.'

'Except Valium. I know you hid them but she tucked a few away.'

'Well, they won't hurt her for a while. She sleeps soundly. All the complaining, I suppose you'd call it, is her way of coping with her fears and physical deprivations. She lives in dread of coming in contact with a snake. I find myself looking around everywhere. There must be so many about yet you don't see them.'

'All jungle creatures are pretty well camouflaged. Roughing it has been hard on Leigh but it hasn't affected your good humour or your beauty.'

'Oh, hasn't it?' Sara smiled. 'There were a few times today I felt like telling Leigh to get lost.'

'I would have put it rather more rudely than that. Sara, you are going to stay with us, aren't you?'

'Well . . .'

'Don't disappoint me, for God's sake,' he begged her. 'Besides, we have a story to tell. It should hit all the papers. You're a journalist. They'll be wanting to hear from you.'

'I guess they will,' Sara agreed cautiously. She wouldn't put it past Evan to try to bounce back jauntily into her life.

'Guy will come out of it the hero.'

'We'll all come out of it pretty well,' Sara murmured thankfully. 'All we need now is for Jake to be OK.'

'I'm just worried Leigh is going to persist with that "It's all your fault!" stuff. You don't know her old man. He eats people alive.'

'Guy will be able to handle it.'

'Don't fall for Guy, Sara. I'm warning you. Leigh
is just kidding herself he's interested in her, but there
are others. Plenty of others. These big tough guys turn
the women on in droves and this one is loaded.
Damned if he hasn't got more than old Sutton, and,
unlike that old bastard, he's never been known to lie
or cheat. He treats everyone right. Even me.'

'Why do you say that?' Sara shifted so that she
could look into Wayne's appealing face. 'For a highly
gifted man you have a surprisingly poor self-image.'

'Don't I ever!'

'Why?' Sara flicked her wildly springing mane back
from her face.

'I'm insecure, I suppose. I was dependent on my
parents, my mother in particular, for a long time. I
don't expect people to feel about painting as I do. It's
my *life*. I've never been any good at anything else. I
was no achiever at school. My mother is the only
person who believed in me from the beginning. My
Dad was great, he left me free to work, but I know
he was always disappointed in me. I wasn't the son
he wanted, even if he went to great lengths to cover
up. I wish he were alive to see I've finally made it.'

'Yes, Wayne, I know how you feel.'

'You're a source of great comfort to me, Sara.'
Wayne lifted her hand and kissed it. 'As far as I'm
concerned, Woman is God's noblest creation, not
Man.'

'What are you two talking about so earnestly?'
Leigh asked sulkily.

'Us.' Wayne turned on her with raised brows.

'How you love your little joke.'

Sara sprang up suddenly. 'We were just speculating
on the sort of reception we'll receive.'

'I see.' Leigh thrust her hand nervously through her
short, dark hair. 'They mustn't take photographs. I
look frightful.'

'You do.'

'You don't look much better.' Leigh picked up a piece of wood and hit Wayne on the shoulder. 'You look as if you've been dragged through the bush backwards.'

'So do you. The camera will be kind to Sara, though. She still has her looks intact.'

'You're unspeakably vicious, Wayne.' Leigh's thin shoulders drooped suddenly and the fire went out of her dark eyes.

'What's the matter with you, I'm *joking*!'

'Why don't you wash your hair in the morning, Leigh?' Sara suggested.

'I *do* look horrid.'

'You'll feel much better.' Sara moved off, but Wayne remained with Leigh and when Sara looked back they were talking quietly. From a psychoanalyst's point of view it was probably a love-hate.

They passed an uneasy night. Guy's absence affected everybody as though without him they had lost not only leadership and direction, but safety. All of them were doubly conscious of the snake menace, and every loud rustling from the thick undergrowth awakened fears of wild boars with their upcurving yellow tusks. Even with rescue at hand, Leigh appeared almost distraught, and with the menfolk fed up, Sara did her best to calm and reassure her. Leigh, out of her protected environment, was as helpless as a canary in the bush.

Their sleep was cut short by a brief but heavy downpour shortly towards dawn. A magnificent flock of galahs, pink and grey cockatoos, screeched loudly in ecstasy, taking to the skies and wheeling in perfect formation over the newly washed trees.

'This is horrible, *horrible*!' Leigh, wet and bedraggled, burst into tears.

'Might as well take a dip,' Sara advised her. 'We couldn't be much wetter than we are.'

'Why not?' Wayne stripped off his wet shirt. 'Don't the eucalypts smell glorious after the rain? It's like floating nectar.'

Sara was more concerned with her stockpile of twigs and fallen branches for the fire. She had left them in a tidy mound but the downpour had soaked and flattened it. She would have to hunt up some more a little back from the camp where the thick canopy of trees would have withstood the rain. A lovely soft breeze had sprung up and the birds had begun their wild, majestic song. Neither Wayne nor Leigh was in the least shy. Certainly not of one another. Leigh was wading in the pool in a flimsy bra and briefs and Wayne was standing waist-high in the water watching her. With the early morning sun on the water, it was a brilliant scene, a symphony of greens with flowering pinks and creams. It was one of the last truly great wilderness areas on the continent and Sara thought she would always carry the spirit of it in her heart.

Jake had stripped off his shirt and was sunning himself on a rock and Sara went to him and gripped his shoulder. 'How are you this morning, Jake?'

There were deep, dark circles beneath Jake's eyes and his skin had a greyish tinge that Sara didn't like. 'Holding my own,' he smiled gamely. 'I hate to think I'm no use to you, Sara.'

'So what do I have to do?' Sara asked him. 'Cook the breakfast. No big deal. I haven't got a lot to offer, though. In a couple of days we all seem to have lost a considerable amount of weight. All protein and lots of exercise. It's good to see Wayne and Leigh enjoying a few minutes together.'

'You'd never guess they were once engaged,' Jake joked. 'I figure Miss Sutton is ahead on points, and even if it came to bare knuckles she'd win.'

'I think, underneath, she's going through a private hell,' Sara said reflectively. 'From all accounts her father is a pretty tough character.'

'You bet!' Jake agreed with a pained expression. 'He's one of those big, overweight guys with freezing eyes and a barely civil manner. He came out of no-where to the north about ten years ago. Plenty of family money, plenty more he made. He's deficient on charm but when it comes to business he's no dummy. In fact he's one of the north's shrewdest op-erators. When we get back I'm going to stay as far away from him as I can. If you think the girl can play hell, you want to meet the father!'

'As bad as that?' Sara's eyes were on the sparkling water.

'I figure all we have to do is stay behind Mr Trenton and let him do the talking. He's streets ahead of Sutton in every department, and that includes big business. Trenton's a man in the old, glorious tradition. Rhodes scholar, brilliant engineer, yachtsman, pilot, been known to raise all sorts of hell in his younger days, promised his father he'd hold on to the plantation but figured he had to do a lot more besides. He was a millionaire many, many times over by the time he was thirty, I think. Couldn't be more than thirty-four now.'

'You'd think some woman would have caught him by now.' Sara shook back her damp mane.

'Plenty have tried, including Miss Sutton there. Gosh, isn't she skinny! Thinks Daddy can buy her a husband, though she knows how to look good when she's dressed right. There was one girl—Annabel something. She made the sparks fly. We thought she'd come out of it Mrs Trenton but something went wrong. Good looker, too, as you'd expect. That white hair—platinum, don't they call it?—and strange light eyes. She also had a husband at one time. Maybe that was it. A man likes a woman all to himself.'

'No argument,' Sara agreed wryly.

'How did you get involved with Palmer, Sara, if you'll forgive my asking? You and I have become good friends.'

'What makes you think we *are* involved?' Sara gazed back at him for a few seconds.

Jake coloured and shrugged apologetically. 'I think the world of you, Sara. You've had a punishing time and not a peep out of you. You work quietly and without complaint. You've done everything in your power to make me feel comfortable.'

'Yes, so why are you worried about Wayne?'

'Did I say I was worried?' Jake hedged.

'No, but you implied it,' Sara concluded. 'I'm not involved with Wayne, Jake. We became friendly after I interviewed him for a programme I worked on. I admire him as an artist and I was quite happy to know a little more about his background.'

'A lot of people up north used to call him a failure,' Jake said unhappily. 'His father was a great bloke, a hard worker. Wayne chose to do nothing but paint. I've always found him very likeable but he does have a few noticeable defects.'

'Don't we all?'

'Don't be angry with me, Sara,' Jake said. 'If you don't know Palmer all that well, forewarned is fore-armed as they say. He's not good enough for you in my estimation.'

'Ah, but then you think I'm near perfect,' Sara returned. 'Wayne invited me for a short visit. I was at a loose end. I'm rarely in this part of the world, so I came. I certainly got more than I bargained for.' That was careless and open to misinterpretation so Sara put her hand on Jake's arm. 'Crazy as it seems, I wouldn't have missed this experience in the rain-forest for the world. It's glorious. It fascinates me. Could anything be more beautiful than this pool? Can any orchestra approach the symphony of the birds?'

Jake's strained face creased into a smile. 'It's fairly obvious it agrees with you. You're a very unusual girl.'

'I know too well.' Her eyes glinted emerald.

'I wouldn't interest myself too much in Palmer's affairs. Try to help him, I mean.'

'Let's get at this thing clearly. What are you trying to say, Jake?'

'Nothing.' Jake seemed in two minds whether to pursue the subject. 'Mrs Palmer is a nice woman but very preoccupied with her only son. She'd recognise straight off you're a giving kind of woman, but a woman who could handle lots of conditions in life.'

'So you're warning me off Mrs Palmer as well?'

'Oh, well,' Jake lowered his head again, looking worried. 'It may be helpful for you to know——'

'What I'm letting myself in for?'

Jake sighed deeply. 'Forgive me, Sara. I'm an interfering old fool.'

'I know you mean well, Jake, but I know how to look after myself, make no mistake.'

'I have a feeling in my bones we're going to be rescued pretty early,' Jake mused, lying back. 'Mr Trenton's such a strong guy he'll endure anything to get us out, and if anyone could help him it would have to be that aboriginal. They're great bushmen.'

'So why don't I get a cup of tea going?' Sara sprang up, slapping bracken off her jeans. 'I'll have to scout around for some dry wood. My little stockpile got drenched.'

'Scout around *where*?' Jake sat up, frowning.

'Don't worry, not far. Back a bit under the trees.'

'Let Palmer do it.' Jake crossed his arm over his chest.

'You're in pain, Jake, aren't you?' Sara sprang back instantly, clutching his shoulder.

'No. A bit of a stab. It's passed off.'

'Sit down, Jake. Don't lie down. Back into the shade.' She helped him.

'I'm so bloody angry, I'm helpless.'

'There. Didn't you say we'd get rescued today?' Sara coaxed him back to comfort. 'I'm not going to do

anything stupid, Jake. That's a promise. I'll just scoot
off and find some wood. You'll be all the better for
a cup of tea.'

Jake nodded and sat there with his head bowed.

Sara carried a shoulder-bag and a long stout stick to
beat the undergrowth. The downpour had been so
heavy the open floor of the forest was covered with
small bunches of berries in brilliant blues and reds,
fallen fruit from the trees. Three or four times she
was hit on the head by debris dislodged by the action
of the wind. She would have to move back further to
find anything dry, but once she did it would take only
seconds to fill her bag. The many species of cuscus
and possums spent the night stripping the trees of old
timber and sending the dry bark to the ground. All
she had to do was keep the water in sight, and that
wasn't difficult as the sun was dancing over its glassy
surface.

All around her the birds continued in full chorus,
and she paused frequently to catch sight of their brilliant plumage. She had never seen such intensity of
colour. There was the most wonderful purple-crowned
pigeon with patches of pink and gold and wings and
tail of an intense green. Wayne painted these birds
beautifully. His 'Creatures of the Rain-Forest' series
had been enormously successful. She had been
somewhat surprised to hear Jake speak out against
him. Obviously in his weakened condition some things
had been preying on Jake's mind. With someone else
she might have told them to mind their own business,
but Jake had adopted a very protective attitude towards her. Sick as he was, he had come between Leigh
and Sara more than once.

Dry wood. Plenty of it. Sara reached for it and as
she did so she was startled by a kind of booming noise.
She stood up quickly and looked around her.

Nothing.

She moved a few yards away. There was plenty of wood. The quiet booming continued. She couldn't tell where it was coming from. Ahead or behind her. It was faintly frightening. She began to move quietly herself and now she realised her movements were being matched by something in the forest. What?

Her eyes tried to pierce the screen of giant ferns in the foreground. It was very difficult to see anything in the forest except the brilliantly coloured birds and butterflies. Snakes and lizards were invisible and the possums were fast asleep in their hollows.

Still, she was being stalked, and by something big.

She was almost on the nest when a great bird raced out from a patch of dense vegetation. To Sara's frightened eyes it was as tall as herself, black-feathered and flightless and brilliantly coloured on the head, neck and wattles.

She had no idea what she had done but every nerve screamed at her that the heavy dangerous bird was on a hard, straight attack. Its neck was stretched forward and it was coming at great speed.

Sara dropped the bag and ran. She knew now it was a cassowary, one of the biggest birds of the world, and somehow unwittingly she had trespassed on its territory, perhaps even the nest. It thundered after her, for all its great weight, far more than her own, and Sara felt her throat pinch in panic. If it ran her down it would savage her with beak and claws.

There was a massive fig tree down a slope she could climb. That was if she had time. She could feel the huge black bird looming up behind her and terror electrified her feet. She homed in on the tree and began pulling herself up by the great woody vines...reaching for another...another...blessing their existence.

The tree was radiant with orchids but she was much too agitated to appreciate their ethereal presence. Finally she judged herself safe. The golden green glow through the trees illuminated the glossy black shape of the bird. It stood motionless, head cocked, an enamelled blue and red, trying to sense her presence, and Sara thought it possible it could even hear her heartbeat like a blacksmith's hammer on the anvil.

A cold sweat trickled down her back and racking shudders clamped the muscles of her stomach.

'You're safe . . . *safe*,' she told herself, trying desperately to gather her resources. 'Breathe slowly, deeply . . . all you have to do is wait it out.'

Finally the bird was satisfied she no longer presented a threat. It turned away with an indignant rumbling and began stomping back through the forest with its stocky, giant stride.

'God, oh my God!' Sara gave a sobbing little laugh of relief. She allowed several more minutes to go by then she decided she had to risk getting back to the camp. It would be harder to get down than it had ever been getting up. Fear truly did lend wings.

The booming and rumbling had stopped. A scratch ran from her wrist to her elbow, welling blood. She grasped a woody vine and began to lower herself carefully down the tree. There was something slimy, shiny, on the next branch. A snake!

She swung out wildly, locking her feet around the vine, her eyes raking frantically for another purchase. Her feet touched, settled on a smaller branch, but as it began to take her weight it snapped off abruptly from the main trunk and taking Sara with it crashed to the ground.

She came to in a fern-filled channel, so much in pain she was afraid it would be impossible to get to her feet. Curiously, her first thought was of Guy. This wouldn't have happened had he not left them. She looked up and saw magnificent new fern fronds waving over her and beyond them a piercing blue sky.

She moved and felt dazzled, violently ill. The realisation of her own weakness was devastating and with

the loss of mobility came wave upon wave of panic.
Suppose they couldn't find her? She appeared to have
rolled much further down the slope, coming to rest
in what looked like an old water channel. Probably
in the monsoon season it would be the bed for a raging
torrent.

She heard voices, Wayne calling for her, but he was
bearing away from her. She returned the call,
wretchedly demanding of her injured body a new burst
of strength, enough energy at least to sit up and yell.
She couldn't think beyond that.

She heard another voice and imagined it was Guy.
A hallucination from the blow on her head. She could
feel the lump by its throbbing.

Now!

She thrust up violently but black spots swam before
her eyes. She tried to move further but the pain in
her left leg had her falling back semi-conscious. She
had broken it. Of course.

She wavered back into consciousness abruptly,
knowing the sound that had aroused her was the loud
whirring of a helicopter. In this remote, silent place
the noise of it was deafening, but she had never heard
anything more welcome in her life. The pain she was
experiencing became more bearable, a shot of adrenalin to dull her misery. All she had to do was lie and
wait for them to find her, and this time she would
have saved up enough voice to lead them to her hidden
gully. A dragonfly with eyes as green as hers hovered
above her and her face was tickled by the wealth of
delicate little ferns that thickly carpeted the channel
and densely matted its sides. Everything was damp:
orchids, mosses, ferns. She was lucky it wasn't the
wet season, otherwise she would have drowned. She
had hit her head on a silver-barked tree stump, its
solidity hardly comparable with the huge granite
boulders in the area. Life had never seemed more
beautiful.

*   *   *

When Guy found her she was lying quietly, eyes bright, face deadly pale, her beautiful red-gold hair flowing over the moss-green ground.

'Sara!' The force of his emotions stopped him.

'I knew you'd come.'

'Don't talk.' He dropped swiftly into the gully, bending over her prostrate form.

As his hands travelled over her, she winced and a muscle pulled tautly along his hard jaw. 'You've broken your leg, I'm afraid.'

'Could have been worse!' she smiled awkwardly, never more aware of his strength and power.

'Well, your ordeal is over.' He looked away from her injured limb and into her eyes. 'I've had the feeling for the last hour that you were in trouble.'

'I'm not now.' Her laugh came in a sharp little spasm. 'Before I passed out I thought you were calling me.'

He cupped her face very slowly and gently. 'Because I *was*. Whether you wanted it or not, Sara, there is a bond between us.'

They were greeted jubilantly by the rescue team, and the media, who hung on Guy's every word. There were very few survivors of jungle crashes, and Sara's own network had sent Evan to meet her. He was genuinely ecstatic that she was alive. In fact he had covered her hand with kisses as she lay on the stretcher waiting to be whisked away to hospital. She and Jake shared the ambulance, both of them responding to the early treatment they had received.

'I've never had this sort of reception in my life,' Jake said shakily. 'I just hope nothing happens to spoil it.'

It was a remarkable time. Everyone wanted to know about their terrifying experience and Sara was glad she was shielded by the hospital. Evan, in fact, was refused permission to visit her room and it was only afterwards that Sara discovered Guy had given the original order.

'Since when do you speak for me?' she challenged him when he came to look in on her.

'Since your legs can't support you,' he returned blandly. 'The doctor tells me you're stuck good and proper for the next six weeks.'

'Stuck where?' She stared up at him as though she thought him a master manipulator.

'I'll be damned if I'll let you go home without seeing the plantation.' He raised his strongly marked, winged brows.

'My mother's coming.'

'I know,' he smiled mockingly. 'I'm picking her up at the airport. We had a long conversation.'

'Oh?' Her injury had made her intensely vulnerable, otherwise she would have been gritting her teeth at his outrageous autocracy. 'Did you speak to my father?'

'I did,' he confirmed rather tersely. 'You have nothing whatever to do but mend.'

'What about Wayne? It pleases you to keep everyone away from me.'

He spread his hands. 'At least until you were over the worst of it. He's dying to see you, of course. And Kirkman is still here, for that matter.'

'I'm perfectly capable of handling Evan.'

'Of course. It's only occasionally you welcome intrusions into your life.'

She had the grace to blush and when she looked up it was to find him studying her with speculative and mocking eyes. 'Back to civilisation, Sara? Back to confronting domineering monsters?'

'There are enough of them about to keep me continually busy.'

He stood up and laughed. 'My dear, you've got me badly miscast.'

She thought he was going to pat her hand but he effectively silenced her by dropping a beautifully controlled kiss on her open, upturned mouth. 'Try to keep in mind I have your best interests at heart.'

'Thank you,' she said crisply, attempting to short circuit his magnetic waves. 'I hope you're going to allow Wayne to look in on me later.'

'The minute he presents himself.' He looked staggeringly, breathtakingly bold and handsome. '*Ciao*, flower-face.'

Leigh, to her surprise, arrived with roses.

'How are you, Sara?'

'Fine. How nice of you to visit me.'

'You've had a terrible time.' Leigh, miraculously restored to the cool social charmer, perched on the bed. 'They tell me Evan Kirkman is waiting to visit you. I'd like to meet him.'

'Why not?' Sara agreed gently, realising Leigh, flawlessly made up and dressed, had probably come to the hospital to do just that. 'You look wonderful. All well-being restored?'

Leigh shuddered and rolled her dark eyes in horror. 'I'll never forget it to the day I die. Guy persuaded Daddy there was absolutely no question of pilot error. I know *I* thought it was Jake's fault, but I hear he's quite seriously ill.'

Sara's heart lurched in dismay. 'But Guy said all he wanted was rest. It was only a mild heart-attack and he's being treated.'

'Oh well, maybe that was it.' Leigh waved the whole issue away carelessly. 'Daddy said he's never lived through such nightmare. I've never in my life seen him cry but there were tears in his eyes when he embraced me.'

'It's a great measure of a man's love when he cries.'

'Do you mean that? You sound odd.'

'Of course I mean it.' Sara turned her head and smiled. 'You adore your father, don't you?'

'He's the most important person in my life.'

'Your mother must feel a little out of it.'

'Mother and I aren't all that compatible,' Leigh said eventually. 'She's had a way of dissociating herself from Daddy and me, yet she loves me, I know.'

'Perhaps she saw your father wouldn't share you.'

'What an extraordinary thing to say. Goodness me!'

'Not in the least. It's almost predictable when one parent is quite dominant. My own father never allowed anyone else to direct my life. No doubt that's why I turned out a rebel.'

'Are you?' Leigh was staring at her in a kind of unwilling admiration.

'Yes, indeed, with plenty of causes.'

'Not the least of which is to find a rich husband.' Leigh's laugh was a little forced.

'Not really.' Sara took it smoothly. 'Like you, I've been used to money all my life.'

'You mean you're an upper-class working girl?'

'In the good old feminist tradition. The Queen has a job. Doesn't she do it superlatively? Don't you wish you could get one?'

'Doing what?' Leigh actually winced. 'There's simply no *need* to work. Most jobs are so terribly common.'

'Sara, ducky!' A male voice called from the door and Evan Kirkman, pink carnations in hand, strode into the room. Ten minutes in the tropical sun had gilded his smooth skin and he looked extraordinarily good-looking. 'My dearest girl.' He bent over and kissed her.

Behind him Leigh silently raised her eyebrows and Sara, after a few seconds, introduced them.

Evan smiled the smile viewers saw every night, quirking his mouth and crinkling his blue eyes. He reacted instantly to a good-looking woman and Leigh, if she wasn't exactly pretty, was very chic and elegant.

'May I say how much I enjoy your programme? I never imagined I would ever meet you.'

'I saw you briefly of course when you were brought in.' Evan was near astonished by the transformation. 'I hope you don't have to rush off. There are quite a few things left to say.' The sun through the window shone on his smooth, thick hair.

For ten minutes or more Sara endured their light flirtation, then Sister came to shoo them off.

Sara was asleep when her mother arrived, opening her eyes when a light hand touched her shoulder and a beloved voice called her name.

'Mummy!' she exclaimed, looking and sounding little more than fourteen years old.

'My precious girl!' Tears in her eyes, Paula Richardson bent over her daughter and rained little kisses over her temples, cheek and nose. 'I've prayed and prayed!'

It was an emotional reunion, each acknowledging their deep-seated fear that somehow, some way they could lose each other. Perhaps in time Sara would overcome the anxieties engendered by her childhood but her mother, with an inborn diffidence, could not change. Both women had been ruled by a man with a genius for creating insecurities and tensions.

'Your father sends his love.' Paula now addressed her daughter warmly but always with that underlying plea for tolerance and understanding. 'He was quite unable to work all the time you were missing, and he has a very big case on at the moment.'

Sara sighed. She invariably found herself saddened by the docility of her mother's nature. Her mother had never asserted herself once in her married life. In many ways her development had been painfully stunted by her early marriage to a very strong and domineering character. She accepted her life, an acceptance springing out of her sincere belief in the sanctity of marriage and the fact that she still, despite his harshness, loved her husband. Sara, the born rebel, was baffled and upset by her mother's quietly resigned responses, but it was hardly the time to lash out now.

They drew together, fingers twined, talking quietly, but once again Sara's heart twisted as she looked at her mother.

Paula Richardson was an extraordinarily beautiful woman, at forty-four at the peak of mature beauty. She wore a white linen suit that emphasised her slender figure and as always, even after a long flight, was the epitome of the immaculately dressed society woman. One would have thought with so much going for her she would have been ultra-confident, but those very close to her like Sara and her two dearest women friends could have attested to her powerlessness. Paula Richardson was humble as few very beautiful women are humble.

'I must say how much I like and admire your Mr Trenton,' Paula now exclaimed almost reverently. 'He met me at the airport and brought me here. So cultured, so charming. For a big, bold, handsome man he has just the right touch with women. One can easily see how his strength saved the day. I've never actually met a hero before.'

'Father has. Met him, I mean.'

'Yes, I *know*!' Paula opened wide her beautiful, blue eyes. 'I think that was one reason why your father refused to give up hope. He recalled Mr Trenton—Guy—vividly. You know how your father comes down on people? He was very impressed when they met. I believe they became quite friendly over dinner. Anyway, knowing it was *he* took a great load off your father's mind.'

'It takes one *man* to spot another.'

'Darling.' Paula took her daughter's hand and stared into her eyes. 'We both know, in many ways, your father is an austere man, but he does love you.'

'In his own way.'

'Some people can't acknowledge love,' Paula pointed out gently.

'Is love really the right word?' Sara lay there quietly. 'Daddy owns us both. Owned us both. He doesn't own me.'

'What can I do, Sara?' Paula asked her. '*I* love him.'

'I know,' Sara smiled into her mother's eyes. 'I'm not absolutely clear why, but I accept that you do. You're like one of the famous heroines of fiction. You're unswervingly loyal. It's too much for me.'

'Ah, I know my girl. You have an enormous capacity for loyalty,' Paula said. 'You just haven't fallen in love, that's all. Have you?'

'What does that mean?'

Paula gave a delicious little gurgle. 'Guy Trenton is enough of a man for any woman. Even you, my little fire-eater. Oh, I can see my own mother in you. She had exactly your spirit. I know she always found me the little mystery in her life. "Dear one, there's absolutely no *need* for you to allow Miles to rule you." She always worried about Miles. To a certain extent she opposed my marriage, but I was so madly in love!'

'It's fairly normal at nineteen. I don't think I'll consider marriage for another four years yet, and maybe not even then.'

'Love's powerful.'

'Mmm!' Sara murmured derisively, but there were strange glints in her eyes.

'What about Wayne Palmer?' Paula asked. 'I had the impression from Guy that he had asked you to stay at the plantation. I'd definitely take him up on it. He's exactly the kind of man I'd adore for a son-in-law.'

'He has lots of lady friends,' Sara pointed out drily. 'You have rather a thing about marrying me off to the right man, haven't you?'

'We-ell, yes.' Paula laughed. 'I know having a career is terribly chic, but a woman on her own is never right.'

'At least she's her own boss,' Sara exclaimed. 'Women have changed, Mummy. We're not Nervous Nellies any more.'

'Most career-women would change places with a happily married wife and mother,' Paula observed neatly, and smoothed a hand over her glorious hair.

'I guess. But I'd rather be on my own, devoting myself to my ambitions, than subordinate to some male. I don't know what I'm going to do about Wayne. His mother invited me to stay with them and I certainly don't want to be a burden. I'll have this cast on for six weeks. It scarcely makes for the ideal house-guest and there's something else.'

'What?' Paula asked with great interest.

'I've decided I don't know Wayne at all.'

'But weren't you trying to get to know him?'

Sara managed to laugh. 'Let's say I learnt *enough* in the last few days. Wayne is a fine artist but I'd rather keep him at arm's length as a man.'

'But he's rather attractive, isn't he? He came over very well on that interview. In fact *I* would have liked to know more as well. He's the sort of man lots of women are drawn to. A kind of little boy lost.'

'I couldn't undertake to help him find himself,' Sara said. 'I like a man to be strong.'

'Then, darling, don't be cross if he can't knuckle down to you as well. Man must be master.'

'Oh, *Mummy*!'

'I told you you'd be cross with me.'

'I'm never cross with you, I love you too much. You're *my* baby.'

Paula lowered her head. 'It often seemed like that, I know. Oh, yes. I'd almost forgotten to mention it. Guy recognises I want to be with you. He's invited me to stay for a week, at least. I know your father won't mind. He has heaps to get through and he dislikes being disturbed.'

'He's a proper little organiser, isn't he?' Sara exclaimed with a flash of something more like panic than irritation.

'I rather like the idea,' Paula said. 'I've never even seen a tea plantation.'

'I couldn't offend Mrs Palmer, though she might be happy to get out of the whole thing. I'll be hobbling around for ages and I don't want her to have to wait on me.'

'Then couldn't you discuss it with Wayne?' Paula suggested. 'I'm quite sure he would understand.'

CHAPTER SIX

WAYNE was torn between dismay and relief at the proposed change of plans. It was one thing to have Sara stay with them as an able-bodied young woman willing to share the load, and another to have to act as nurse. His mother was convinced she could cope, but the only burden she had ever been asked to tote was her son.

So it was decided. Sara could have gone back with her mother, of course, but she could no longer bear to live at home. In fact it was much easier for her mother to manage with her father alone. Sara's fighting spirit created tensions, whereas Paula had long since learnt to obey a clear set of rules. Sara had come to the north for a well earned holiday, and she was incapacitated anyway. Though Mrs Palmer was very comfortable in her home, there was a whole world of difference between her resources and Guy Trenton's. One didn't feel so badly about imposing on a rich man, and he had assured Paula he was all eager-ness to supply diversions.

'You'll come and visit us though, won't you?' Wayne asked, aggrieved.

'Of course. I would want to explain to your mother in person.'

'It's quite monstrous, isn't it, the way things have gone?'

'I could hardly think so, Wayne.' Sara stared at him. 'Our lives have been spared.'

'Oh, I don't mean that!' Wayne turned from the window to face her. 'I mean your breaking your leg. There were so many things I wanted us to do.'

'I can stomp around,' Sara pointed out drily. 'You know, like a big bird. I'll never forget that cassowary racing after me. I couldn't have been more frightened if it had been an elephant about to flatten me.'

'I came after you, you know.'

Sara looked back at him with her sparkling green eyes. 'I heard you call. It's just that you were going the wrong way.'

'Ah well, Trenton's the good-guy material. I thought he was going to punch me when he found you were missing. I'm certain he almost did. You would have thought it was my fault you wandered off. It seemed unreasonable, even irrational, to me. He didn't ask anyone to join him. He just charged off.'

What a mercy! Sara thought but didn't say.

She left the hospital flanked by Guy Trenton and her mother.

'Darling, this is exciting!' Paula fluted in her ear. She reached forward from the back seat of the big Mercedes to tap Guy's shoulder lightly. 'How far to the plantation, Guy?'

'You sound like a little girl!' He showed them his rugged profile. 'Both you and Sara have the sweetest laugh. Young and innocent.'

Paula blushed and pressed her daughter's hand.

'About twenty miles.' Guy put the car in gear. 'One stop to pick up a parcel and we'll be there.'

'I can't wait.' Paula picked up Sara's hand and pressed her soft-petalled lips to it. 'My own girl! We haven't had a holiday together in ages.'

Just a little kid out of school. Sara looked up and caught Guy's perceptive eyes in the rear-view mirror. It was obvious he liked her mother—who wouldn't? But he could see Sara had not modelled herself on Paula. Sara's character was shaped by inherited char-acteristics and the way she had been treated. One parent she was fiercely protective of; the other called up a whole arsenal of defences. It seemed increasingly strange that Guy had had contact with her father and no doubt had formed opinions of his own. 'Marvelous conversationalist, controversial.' There was no doubt about it, her father presented an excellent front. Sara didn't realise it, but her eyes were flashing sparks.

The plantation was like a dream; the emerald-green slopes covered with row upon row of compact glossy bushes, filling the visible world and dominated by a purple mountain peak that thrust a fantasy finger up from the brilliant rain-forest. A single white cloud scudded across it in shining contrast to the blue-flame sky and an avenue of jacarandas, a miracle of lavender blossoms, ran a quarter of a mile to the plantation house door.

'Why, words can't describe it!' Paula gasped. 'This is glorious country, Guy!'

'I've never seen any more beautiful in the world and I've been everywhere. Nature is at its lushest, its most prolific in the tropics and we're high enough up to miss the worst of the heat.'

'I've never seen such green! A quite different green from the temperate climates. It has such a marvellous brilliance.' Paula turned enthusiastically to her daughter. 'You'd be able to write here.'

'Finish your book,' came Guy's reply.

'So you know about it?' Paula tore her eyes from the beautiful, luminous scene.

'Guy is one of those people who come to know everything,' Sara said.

The plantation house was just as a novelist might imagine it, perhaps even built on a more magnificent scale. It was very big, designed and built as a tropical mansion; single-storeyed and enclosed by wonderfully spacious verandas. It was painted white, but instead of elaborate cast-iron lacework, some marvellous craftsman had used timber for the balustrading, the carved caps and fretwork on the gables. Big as it was, it was beautifully proportioned following Georgian symmetrical patterns, the whole set off by the very extensive home gardens. In late spring it was a glory, with spectacular strands of splendid flowers such as neither woman had seen before in their lives.

Paula, a most enthusiastic gardener—indeed it was an area of great release for her—was in the seventh heaven.

'Slow down, Guy. Oh, *please*. What was that?' She indicated a large stand of fantastic ten-inch enamel-red flowers standing tall on cane-like stems.

'Torch ginger.' Guy slowed the car to a near halt to oblige her. 'One of the great flowers of the world. It's originally from Indonesia.'

'I *must* have it.'

'My dear, you won't get it to grow away from the tropics unless you have a greenhouse, and I'd say it was much too big. Most of the flowers here were selected to suit the tropical conditions and for dramatic effect. Our light demands brilliant colours. Pastels would bleach into nothingness, although as you can see there are masses and masses of tropical orchids, bromeliads and lilies beneath the trees. There's a particularly gorgeous tropical plant you could try in some sheltered spot, the medinilla.'

'And where's that?'

'Up ahead.'

'Not those fantastic hanging flower clusters?'

'I can see you're going to have a wonderful time walking around the garden,' Guy laughed. 'We'll have to push Sara between us.'

'You're too good to me, Guy,' Sara smiled at him coolly.

'Why should I not be?' His topaz eyes gleamed. 'It's not every day a man has two such beautiful women under his roof.'

Now people were running across the plush emerald grass. 'Oh-oh, my welcoming party,' Guy muttered.

Paula waved her hand. 'They must be thrilled to have you safely back.'

'Looks like it.' He gave a warm laugh. 'My Aunt Clare will be staying with us, a chaperon for Sara when you go, Paula. She too adores her garden, so you'll have a lot in common. The others waving so madly are all staff. Esther, my housekeeper. She's been with my family most of her life. Tom, her husband, is the manager. The fellows in a ring work around the estate in various capacities.'

'Do all of them kneel at your feet?'

'Sara!' Paula said softly.

Guy didn't answer. He didn't appear to notice. He stopped the car in front of the short flight of stone steps and almost immediately the car was surrounded by his 'loyal subjects'.

If only I could walk, Sara thought, as he swooped her up.

His aunt at the top of the stairs held out her arms, beaming. She was sweet-faced, dark-haired, beautiful.

Some men were born to be adored.

'Are you all right, darling? You look a little peaky,' Paula observed after Clare Trenton had smilingly left them in what amounted to a suite of rooms.

'I'm fine.' Sara relaxed in a deep armchair, looking with delight at a four-poster bed hung with filmy draperies. 'What a lovely woman!' she remarked of Guy's aunt. 'I find I have a burning desire to know why she has never married.'

'She looks very much to me like a one-man woman.' Paula smoothed a slow hand over a brass-bound, lacquered chest. 'Maybe she lost him.'

'It shouldn't be. It's too sad.'

Paula disappeared into a huge wardrobe. 'I thought *we* had a big house, but one could get lost here. Did you ever see such wonderful furniture? Indian, isn't it? I'm anxious to find out.'

'There are so many things!' Sara spread her hands.
'Collecting must be a passion with them. I love all
the polished floors and the parquetry and those marvellous rugs! It's the most sensuous house I've ever
been in in my life. The rooms fairly pulse with
exotica. Of course they came from Ceylon, and that
part of the world is well represented here. Did you
notice the paintings and bronzes and those splendid
inlaid chairs? Even the house itself reflects Indian
architecture, slender carved columns and those lovely
filigreed screens.'

'Not to mention the lotus pools. I suppose the
climate is much like Ceylon's—I can never get used
to calling it Sri Lanka. I suppose that's why they chose
it to grow their tea. Don't the hillsides look fantastic,
and that peak, the way it rears itself against the sky!
I've fallen violently in love with the place.'

Clare, who was a most sensible and sensitive
woman, further delighted mother and daughter, who
had moved out on to the veranda contemplating one
of many ornamental lily ponds. She knocked on Sara's
door and came through to join them carrying the most
ravishing array of gorgeous floating fabrics.

'What have we here?' Paula pressed her hands together, staring down at the sculptured folds in Clare's
arms.

'Saris for every occasion!' Clare laughed. 'It seemed
to me it might make things very much easier for Sara.
If she would like to she can simply drape herself in
these.'

'Why, how marvellous!' Sara, with a pronounced
pallor, stumbled suddenly back into a chair.

'Darling!' Paula cried but both women closed in
on her.

'It's all right, I promise,' Sara said lightly. 'Now
and again I feel a bit weak.'

'You mustn't let us tire you,' Clare said. 'Reaction
can come on one without warning. Guy has empha-

sised this. He told me you showed so much courage you might have put quite a drain on your strength.'

'I hope he told you we'd still be going around in circles if we hadn't had him.'

'I know Guy,' Clare murmured. 'Ah, you've got a little of your colour back.'

'What about a sleep, darling?' Paula suggested.

'A little rest wouldn't hurt.' Now Sara realised just how depleted she felt. 'Thank you so much for the saris, Clare. They look gorgeous, and they're exactly what I need.'

'Be sure to lend me one,' Paula smiled, and pressed her daughter's glowing hair back.

'I have one for you, Paula,' Clare promised. 'Honestly, to see you two together is enchanting. You're so much alike! That exquisite colouring! Yet your eyes are a deep blue, Paula, and Sara's are nothing else but green. They remind me of the lily pool with the sun on it.'

It was the start of one of the happiest weeks Sara had ever had in her life. Certainly she had never felt so secure and at peace in her own home. Of course Guy and his wonderful aunt set the mood, allowing their guests all the privacy and freedom they needed, interspersed with delicious meals, and as much sightseeing as Sara could comfortably cope with. They might have been dearest relatives, except for the wildly unsettling looks Guy occasionally gave her. For the most part he could have been her favourite cousin. He was kindness and consideration itself, as was Clare, and both women blossomed in such a warm, carefree atmosphere.

'Honestly, I won't want to go home,' Paula moaned. 'This is Paradise!'

Guy was in and out, a million and one things to fill his day even when he was putting off a good many of his commitments to be on hand to look after his guests.

Sara was relaxing in a beautiful, shady corner of the garden when he loped across the lawn to her with his dancer-athlete's stride, she couldn't decide which, there was so much grace and power.

'How goes it, little one?'

'I can't thank you enough, Guy,' she told him huskily, the deepening green of her eyes in marked contrast to the flame of her hair and her magnolia skin. 'You and Clare have been so terribly kind to us. My mother is blooming. I've never seen her so relaxed and happy.'

'She's a very lovable person.'

'Yes, she is,' Sara agreed and a little bleakness escaped her.

'You're very protective of her, aren't you?' There was room on the plushly upholstered recliner and he sat sideways near her feet.

'She's *my* baby,' Sara smiled.

'And when did you take over the adult role?'

'Now don't you start analysing me.' She veiled her eyes from him. 'It seems to be one of your favourite occupations.'

'What do you expect?' His indulgent drawl was faintly clipped. 'You move around my home like a vision.'

'You mean I'm wheeled around your home or you carry me.'

'I guess I'll miss it when I have to stop. I've never seen a woman look more beautiful in a sari.'

'Not even a dusky Singalese maiden?' For some reason that hurt her.

'You can't imagine how piquant it is, Sara, to see a sari on a creamy-skinned redhead.'

He stared at her across the little space, thick eyelashes veiling his golden eyes.

'There, you've done it again!' she cried out.

'Done what?' The challenge sounded in his voice.

She put her palms against the wooden sides of the recliner, wishing she could simply push up and run away. 'All week you've been giving a marvellous impersonation of Cousin Guy, and the joke is I've been revelling in it. Then out of the blue you give me a look that shatters the illusion to little splinters. I feel like a trusting little doe that's about to be gobbled up by a leopard and probably spat out.'

'My dear!'

'Don't *my dear* me,' she flared.

'You've a rather bad thing about rejection, haven't you? You think all men carry the power principle to extremes?'

'It started thousands of years ago.'

'Are we going to disregard all the hen-pecked husbands?'

'Don't be frivolous, Guy!'

'You want frivolity? I could show you many a man in my employ who's terrified of upsetting his wife. One in particular gets a saucepan over his head every time he stumbles up the front stairs.'

'He knows he shouldn't get drunk.'

'You'd make a pretty formidable "little woman" yourself.'

'Don't be ridiculous.'

'No, let's follow this up,' he said relentlessly. 'You're the one who always starts this sexist stuff.'

'Because I was——'

'What?'

'My God, my God, let's forget it.' She turned her head almost frantically to the side.

'All right.' His eyes were on a perfect face that had gone white. 'You've been living on your nerves all your life. I'm not interested in trapping or controlling you, Sara. I don't have to do anything like that to prove my masculinity. I'm totally against degrading women in any way and I'd like you to consider, *men* have helped women more than women have ever helped themselves.'

'I know!' She sat up and let her head slump over. 'I can't get anywhere with you. You're too clever.'

'So?' He put a hand beneath her chin and lifted her head up, the long, silky strands of her hair curving about his wrist. 'How about putting these little discussions aside until your body's stronger? I know Esther has been trying to feed you up, but you don't seem to have gained even one pound that you lost. You're fragile, Sara, you know that. Not slender, fragile. Don't fight me. I'll wear you out.'

Her eyes glittered with little pinpoints of light. 'I'd never be content with unconditional surrender.'

'I know that. I know all about you.' He tilted his head forward and abruptly kissed her mouth.

'Guy!' It was communication at its most powerful, basic level.

'Yes, Sara?' His voice was as soft as velvet.

'Don't you think someone might come?'

'Just listen to yourself, little one. What are you afraid of?'

'What you do to me.'

'Your body tells you what's right for you.'

'I don't trust it.'

He sat up. 'Would you care for a long friendship first?'

She shook her lustrous head. 'I knew you on sight.'

'As you wish, my lady.' His golden eyes sparkled with mockery. 'These things can't be rushed. What I really came to ask you, Sara, is: do you feel up to a small dinner party tomorrow night? I feel we should have one for your mother. We've all been considering you. You know that. But perhaps the time is just right.'

'Have you spoken to Mummy?' There was instantly a soft flush of colour in her face.

'Not yet.' His glance slanted indulgently over her.
'I take it you'd like that.'

'It'd be fun!'

'Then it's as good as done.' He gave his devastat-
ingly attractive smile. 'I guess I'll have to ask Leigh.'

'Don't you want to?'

'I was thinking of leaving out Palmer.'

'You can't!'

His glance struck her face. 'Missing him, are you?'

'It would be rather cruel to leave him out.'

'What if I've made other arrangements? What if I
have a cruel side you've never seen?'

She shrugged her delicate shoulders. 'What I already know is more than enough.'

'There's no other way to tell you but straight out.
Get involved with Palmer and you're going nowhere.
I haven't just been acting Cousin Guy. I feel a real
responsibility for you. I don't mean to suggest you
can't handle your own life.'

'Oh yes, you do!'

'All right, I *do*. You weren't handling Kirkman
particularly well.'

'Is it possible you're ever going to forget that?'

'Consider I had to get rid of him from the hospital.'

'Because I was bound to a bed.'

'All I'm saying is, don't add to your problems by
becoming the muse to Palmer's genius. He's gifted,
I'll grant you, but I know he would make life very
difficult for a woman. It seems to me you've had
enough stress.'

'You don't know anything about me!' she said bitterly, infuriated by the very high-handedness she had
been known to welcome.

'Don't I?' he said curtly and stood up. 'You're a
battered child.'

She was shocked, realising with sudden shame that
many of her attitudes were a silent scream.

'Guy...'

He looked back at her, tall, dangerous, formidable, his eyes a golden blaze in a stunning face. 'I'm listening.'

'I'm sorry.'

'Not for long.'

'You're a very special person. I'm sorry.'

He gave a sceptical little grunt. 'It's very kind of you to say so.'

Her eyes intolerably began to well with tears.

'Don't *do* that!' He sounded tense.

'It's this leg. It's this plaster.'

'Yes.' He too looked under pressure.

'Oh, I've never had a broken limb in my life.'

'Stop. Just stop, Sara,' he said harshly. 'You have nothing to do but mend, and I'll go back to being your guardian angel.'

Fourteen in all sat down to dinner in the beautiful big living-room with pairs of french doors providing lovely long vistas of the gardens and lily pools. The scent of the night-blooming cereus was in the air, insinuating, intoxicating, wafting with the breeze into the soft opulence of the room.

Sara, in an exquisite jade-green and gold sari, allowed herself to relax and drink it all in. Magnificent inlaid chairs surrounded the highly polished table set with superb hand-painted gold-rimmed china, the crystal fire of glasses, the soft lustre of eighteenth-century English silver. Breathtakingly beautiful orchids, all in delicate shades of white, palest gold and lime-green, graced raised *famille verte* bowls down the length of the table, and fine linen place-mats and matching napkins were wondrously stitched and embroidered.

Guy and Clare were very much at their ease, and their guests gratefully followed such a confident and graceful lead. The men in concession to the heat wore lightweight suits in natural fibres; the women, whisper-thin fabrics in blue, hyacinth, delicate rose and a lovely floral design. Only Sara wore jewel colours, and the richness of her colouring complemented them beautifully.

'You bring a new interpretation to a legendary garment,' Wayne told her ardently. It was obvious he was captivated by a wealth of red-gold hair, creamy skin and emerald eyes, her softly curved form. It was almost as if he hungered to arrange her into a hundred different poses, but in the end he had to be satisfied to sit and admire.

'No doubt about it, Wayne likes you in a sari,' Guy murmured to her sardonically, a faintly menacing arc to his black brows. 'He always did care for a touch of the exotic.'

Dinner made great use of the tropical bounty of seafood and exotic fruits. Prime beef was included on the menu, but everyone was tempted by the sweet-fleshed prawns, rock oysters, marvellous baby lobsters and the superlative Queensland barramundi, rated as among the finest eating-fish in the world. There were several different kinds of salads wonderfully presented and afterwards jade fruits with avocado or coconut ice-cream and a luscious lime cream tart.

It was a highly successful night and afterwards the guests came to Sara to say goodnight. It was rather like holding court, for she reclined on a sofa upholstered in gold silk moiré with piles of betasselled silk cushions at her back.

Wayne renewed his plea for Sara to visit them. 'You've given a whole wider meaning to my life,' he told her intensely. 'One could plan a future with a woman like you. You take life and you live it.'

'I'm glad it seems that way,' Sara said with disarming honesty. 'But I have lots of unresolved conflicts, Wayne.'

'You were the consistently strong one in the days after the crash,' he pointed out undeterred. 'You saw how Leigh broke into little pieces. She was hysterical most of the time, and she's the one who claims she's put together pretty well. Look at her tonight! Did you ever see such a transformation from that pathetic creature in the jungle?'

Sara opened her mouth to argue, then shut it again. 'I was looking forward to a hot soak myself,' she contributed finally. 'Leigh will improve as she gets away from her father. Her mother is a nice woman.'

Wayne muttered a hot exclamation.

Leigh, in fact, was unmistakably jealous. 'A splendid turn-out, Sara!' she clipped off almost furiously.

'*You* couldn't have done it better,' Wayne drawled.

Leigh chose to ignore him, but her heavily mascaraed eyes glittered. 'I'm very impressed with your mother, Sara. A gorgeous-looking woman and she's so warm and friendly.'

'Sara is the *image* of her mother,' Wayne offered maliciously. 'Except for the eyes and a difference in expression. Paula is the angel, but Sara has too much fire and spirit. She could easily get herself into trouble.'

'Exactly, darling. With you,' Leigh shot back.

'And what does that mean?' Wayne asked sharply.

'You're a very disappointing kind of person.'

Sara pushed back further into the cushions. 'Please, not tonight. Why don't you two call a ceasefire? Then again, I suppose you could enjoy fighting. Both of you can be so cruel, yet underneath you really care about one another. Human relationships don't make sense.'

'You can say that again!' Leigh dashed off with a swirl of her rose-coloured skirts.

'We've got to get this straight now, Sara,' Wayne implored her. 'My affair with Leigh is over. Don't stir up the pain.'

'The pain should have dulled!'

'It has!' Wayne caught her hand and carried it to his mouth. 'You've walked into my life and I'm half-way in love with you already.'

'Probably that's as far as you'll get,' Sara suggested. 'Half-way wouldn't be half good enough for me.'

'I admire you, Sara,' Wayne said fervently. 'You're kind and tolerant. Not like that bitch Leigh. You say we care about one another: I dislike her as much as she dislikes me!'

'Fire is one of the real marks of passion.'

'Will you *listen*, Sara? When I first met you I thought: my God, here's a woman to show me the way. I've been floundering so badly, but you walked in with your smile and your strength. A man needs a woman to lean on.'

'*Does* he?' Sara couldn't help looking towards the singularly self-sufficient Guy.

'Don't look at Guy,' Wayne warned her bluntly. 'He's not for you.'

'Maybe not, but he's a mesmerising man.'

'He certainly manoeuvred you into staying here,' Wayne said bluntly. 'Take care, Sara. I'll ring.' He bent over her and, instead of kissing her cheek as Sara anticipated, he aimed for her mouth and kissed it lingeringly.

Handicapped, she was a sitting duck.

Guy made no mention of it until he carried her up to bed. Paula and Clare had long since retired but Guy and Sara had sat on talking over the events of the night and Sara's impressions of his friends. Both of them were aware Paula and Clare were setting the stage for a little romance, and even Sara felt over-whelmed with frustration that she had to be trundled around. She couldn't *wait* for the cast to come off! Casualties weren't romantic, were they?

Having him in her bedroom created a tremendous atmosphere of excitement and tension. Light glanced off his high cheekbones and there was a certain hard watchfulness in his expression.

'Are you sure you're going to be able to manage?'

'Of course.' She sat on the side of the bed, the glowing centre of a pool of light.

'Paula usually helps you.' He looked around as though for her night-clothes.

'Oh, really, Guy,' she said wryly.

'You don't approve of their matchmaking plans?'

'It's not having much effect, is it?'

'What is it you *want*?' He clipped off the syllables.

'I don't want anything. You've been very good to me.'

'Then why not follow my advice?'

'I knew it!' She tossed back her hair. 'I'm in for a lecture.'

'Kissing is usually very private.'

A pulse began to beat in the vulnerable hollow of her throat. 'I don't know. In my circle people are kissing all the time.'

'Am I supposed to believe you don't mind casual affairs?'

'I don't understand you.'

'You're not *that* dumb.'

'*Dumb!*' She was so angry she actually thrust forward, not thinking of her leg, and would have hurtled to the floor if Guy had not caught her.

'Sometimes I think you're going to drive me out of my mind, Trenton.'

'The name is *Guy*.' His golden-amber eyes were mere slits. 'Are you going to come quietly?'

'I think it's pretty noticeable I can't do too damned much at all.'

'Like move your head when Palmer bent to kiss you? You're doing a good job of moving it now.'

She stopped struggling because her heart was beating hurtfully. 'I'm afraid of you, that's why.'

'Funny sort of afraid.' He moved her slender body right up against him, taking her weight. 'You've been giving me the great big come-on from glance one.'

'It's long been known that men kid themselves.'

'Then it's a lie?'

'Aren't you taking advantage of my helplessness?' she challenged him.

'Helplessness?' He laughed, malicious and mocking. 'You'd never be helpless, Sara. I think you'd bite and claw.'

'I certainly would if I were able. You're hurting me, Guy.'

'It's hard to see how.' Nevertheless he scooped her up and set her down once more on the bed. 'I don't think I much care for that expression,' he said, looking down into her lovely mutinous face.

'What expression?'

'You don't even know you're doing it. You're so in the habit of defending yourself, you fail to re-cognise when you don't *have* to. Remember that first day? Your impulse to aggression? It burst out of you. Flashed out of your eyes. You're a well educated young woman. It's about time you broke free of the adolescent struggles. You *know* you overreacted to me. If you don't resolve your conflicts they will lead to conflicts with others. I am *not* your father, Sara. We might have some characteristics in common, but I don't think we could be defined as the same *type*.'

'Both of you have a terrible tendency to dominate.'

'Let me counter that by saying *I* am merely trying to offer some damned good advice. I've had quite a few more years' experience than you. Also, I know Wayne Palmer and the way he reacts to what he calls "artistic stimulation". After years of restraint you

might think you need a man to control rather than
have him control you, but the dependence of a man
like Palmer could push you to the limits. His mother
is concrete evidence of his leaning on women. Leigh
got sick of it, as you've seen.'

'There's a love-hate there!' Sara pointed out with
brilliant eyes.

'Then why don't you leave them to it?' He caught
her chin and made her look at him.

'I have *attempted* to.' With his hand on her skin,
her breath became deep and urgent.

'Forgive me if I disagree. He couldn't keep his eyes
off you all night.'

'He's in love with my *hair*. Not me.' Her hair fanned
around her face in a glorious curtain.

He nodded. 'He must be if he plans to paint your
portrait. But couldn't you keep it professional? I don't
recall seeing you fight shy of a very passionate kiss.'

'Well, I haven't had one for several days.'

'I appreciate that, but I've been doing my level best
to act nobly through your helpless state.'

She flung out her slender arm and turned her
flushed face along it. 'I don't know what's the matter
with me.'

'You'll feel a lot better when that cast is off.' He
said it in such a cool, clinical way that Sara gave a
jagged little moan.

'Goodnight, Guy.' She stared directly at a little car-
riage clock. 'Morning.'

'What's the rush?'

'The discussion is over.'

'Maybe,' he agreed suavely, 'but *I* plan to kiss you
before I go.'

'No, thanks.' She buried her face in the pillow. Her
body was screaming with frustration.

'Come here, my Jade Princess,' he laughed in his
throat. 'Occasionally I go over our first meeting in
detail. I wanted to catch you up then and kiss the

bright challenge off your face. Then I wanted to comfort you. Crazy, isn't it? A woman has never affected me like that before. You want to hurt her and kiss her better all at once.'

He wound her silky hair around his hand and turned her to him, his handsome face drawn with controlled sensuality.

'I don't *want* you to kiss me, Guy.' She considered, if he did, she wouldn't be able to sleep.

'Doctor's orders. Besides, I want to be certain to erase Palmer's.'

They seemed to be at the centre of a highly magnetised field of tension. Sara had no choice but to wait until his mouth came down to cover hers. Only his hand shaped her breast, the creamy column of her throat.

'Don't *do* that!'

'There doesn't seem to be a way I can stop myself. If ever a woman made colours her own, yours are green and gold.'

'What are you doing to me, Guy?' she whispered.

'You'll see.'

'Mummy and Clare——'

'Are fast asleep. Or, as you're perfectly well aware, doing their level best to leave us alone.'

'It's a far cry from the way you've *been* treating me,' she pointed out shakily.

'Don't you like it?'

Her eyelids fluttered. Was he teasing her, tormenting her, what?

'All right, that's enough!' She made herself grip a fold of the sari he was unwinding so skilfully, but to her trembling amazement he caught her wrist.

'Lovely Sara!' There was a slight rasp in his groan.

A spasm of something not unlike fear crossed her face.

'What is it?' he asked huskily. 'I would never hurt you. I'm overwhelmed by your innocence.'

'Innocence?' She never realised she could reveal herself so completely. She didn't want to. 'You don't *know.*'

'Are you going to tell me you were Kirkman's mistress?'

'No. I was not Evan's mistress. I have an idea of myself that wouldn't consider such a role.'

'Good. I like a clear self-image.' His astonishing golden eyes were amused and indulgent. 'Come, I'm only going to make love to you a little. The next time, perhaps a little more. You nurse some feeling for me. I know that.'

She made no move. No sound. Not because the sleeping household was her first concern, but because she could not renounce this strange, tormenting ecstasy. He could arouse her in a way she had never thought herself capable of. Such in fact was her innocence of real physical passion she was even appalled by her own sexuality. From the very first he had confused and shocked her beyond all her experience.

She shivered and he eased her gently back. '*Yes,* Sara,' he told her softly, almost tenderly. 'You have nothing to fear.'

Her breasts were small and round and high, unconfined in the tropical heat.

He made no attempt to touch her, but drew back a little as though he wanted nothing more than to watch the play of light on her beautiful skin.

Seconds . . . yet the effect was dazzling. It was difficult not to *beg* him to touch her, but her throat had tightened so much she could not speak. Her whole body was awash with heat, her veins streams of fire.

'You're shaped *exactly* as I knew you would be.' His long tanned fingers began to trace in fascination the rosy aureoles of her breasts, causing her nipples to tingle and rise into tightly furled erotic buds. Everything he did to her had such an astonishing intimacy it stole her breath away. Her very senses. When she was with him she felt she was entering a world that had always been beyond her. She could not explore it alone. He had to guide her. He was in the position of master and she felt this explained the element of panic in her infinite pleasure.

She had lived in innocence. There was no need to consider her past experiences. One glance from Guy's eyes stirred her more deeply than any kiss, any caress she had ever known.

She didn't realise her beautiful green eyes had clouded.

'Don't weep.' His voice was velvety and gentle, but a tremendous power and male energy emanated from his lean hard body.

'You mustn't do this to me, Guy.'

'I think I must. You've been waiting for it. You're infinitely a woman. The very essence of femininity. Life demands it.' He bent his dark head and began to draw ravishingly on her young breast.

'Guy!' Abruptly, shockingly, her back arched off the bed. She was on fire, shafts of sensation racing down into her groin.

Once started, he chose not to stop.

The pressures that built up in her were immense. She caught his thick dark hair, curling her fingers around crisp, jet-black curls, trying to force his head away from her quivering, yearning body.

'Sara!' It was a long drawn out sigh of sexual desire and it turned her limbs liquid.

There was no question of evading his full, finely sculptured mouth. It came down on hers so strongly, yet so deeply caressing and alive it smothered her tremulous sob. No one had touched her, kissed her like this. He made her feel as though she was infinitely beautiful, not a body to be exploited.

Now she was naked to the waist, but the sari held firm to her hips. She was utterly subdued by his touch, yielding and permissive, as he began to move his hands up and down over her back, her spine, her narrow waist and the curve of her hips.

Everything was lost. Sight, sound, sense. Their very surroundings were eliminated by a fast-rising relentless passion. She wasn't in a room or a bed. She was engulfed in some cocoon-like, secret place where the realities of life had no function. It was rapture, without beginning, without end... Her breasts tingled, not hurtfully, but enough, she knew, to remind her during the following days. Surely such communication went far beyond the physical level? She had a sense of reaching his spirit, his soul.

When at last he released her she cried out at the pain of rejection.

'Hush, Sara.' His voice was very husky. 'I don't want this ever to end. In fact, I'll have to plan things a lot better.'

'*What?*' She stretched out her hand, her emerald eyes huge and bemused.

'I *want* to love you, Sara,' he said bluntly. 'The day is fast coming when I shall. But *you* have to be prepared.'

'For what, annihilation? *You* chose to start this.'

'Yes, I did,' he confessed grimly. 'I'd best get going then. That white skin is incandescent.' He stood up very quickly and moved away.

'Is there any reason why you won't pass me my nightgown and robe?'

'Don't for God's sake ask me to put you in it,' he frowned.

'Are you *angry*?'

His formidable dark face seemed to soften. 'More frustrated than angry. You have a rare magic. Not only that, the spell lingers on. I could almost wish you weren't so pure.'

'Does being pure demand patronising?' she sparkled. 'There could very well be several things I haven't told you.'

'That sounds like a little shout of bravado.'

'Quite right. I don't have to make excuses for my own strength of character. On the other hand, do you make love to all your female guests?'

'Hardly at all. I really haven't been involved with all that many women in spite of the reputation I seem to have been given. Sex without caring isn't my scene.'

'Marriage isn't either.'

'I didn't say I wouldn't *try* it.' Her nightgown and robe were lying over an armchair close at hand and he went to it and picked them up. 'Here.'

She stretched out one hand for her gown and held the green and gold sari demurely to her breasts.

'Little late for that, isn't it? You might think you look maidenly, but you're more like a siren.' He found the low, scooped neckline and dropped it over her glowing head.

'Don't worry. I can fix it,' she muttered, her voice muffled.

'It will be easier if you allow me to help you. That's if I can keep my mind on the job.' As he pulled her arms through the small puffed sleeves his hands touched her breasts.

'And you're the man I thought was always in control of himself.'

'I always have been,' he responded sardonically. 'Going back to before I met you.'

The very fine cotton seemed to graze her nipples.

'Did I hurt you?' he asked almost curtly.

'I *will* notice it.'

'So will I.' His disturbing glance slid over her. 'When are you going to sort out what you feel in your mind?'

'It can't be done overnight,' she said warily, terrified of relinquishing her life to a man.

'You realise, little one, I mightn't be able to stop next time.'

'*Next* time I should be out of this cast,' she said spiritedly. 'It will make it easier to run away.'

'That's something we'll test out.'

'Absolutely.' She swallowed. In fact she was astonished by the audacity she was able to muster.

He didn't appear to take it seriously. 'Can I fill the wash-basin for you?' he suggested, walking towards the adjoining bathroom. 'Put toothpaste on your brush. Find a face-washer? Helpful little things like that?'

'I dare not encourage you,' she said strictly.

'Really?' He turned back to stare at her. 'It wasn't like that a few minutes ago.'

Colour flared through her whole body, lighting her skin. 'You saved my life. I owed you a kiss in return.'

'I got a lot more than that.' His vibrant voice was full of mockery.

'If there *is* a fault, it lies in our chemistry.'

'I agree, Sara,' he said smoothly. 'I suppose we could say, it's *explosive*?'

CHAPTER SEVEN

PAULA went home and the days slipped by as Sara settled into an enjoyable routine. Despite her disability she was determined to find out all she could about plantation life, which surely pleased Guy because he took her with him everywhere.

'I think he's seeing it all afresh through your eyes,' Clare remarked indulgently. 'You have such a bright, enquiring mind. One thing only, don't tire yourself out.'

That would have been difficult. Guy watched over her with the dedication of a brother. In fact it would not have been possible for him to show more care and consideration. It was difficult to hold to the view that all men were monsters when it was manifest that she was being treated like a princess. The only thing Guy and her father had in common was they projected the dynamic male image. Her father exulted in being the ultimate chauvinist. Guy genuinely enjoyed a woman's company. He had an excellent relationship with his aunt, something Sara found tremendously reassuring, and from all accounts his mother and sister, temporarily stationed in London, missed him dreadfully. He was the realisation of a totally integrated human being. There was no terrible on-going fight for near-equality, equality clearly beyond womankind. How could she fight when her rights were clearly recognised? She felt like a dragon with her fire-breathing apparatus put out. Without even knowing it, she had stumbled into Paradise with Adam and Eve treated exactly the same.

Workers on the estate became used to seeing them together: in the fields, the seed gardens, the factory. There was an extensive domestic market and so far supply was a long way behind demand. The tea industry was only in its infancy but just as Australia had successfully mechanised the labour-intensive sugar industry, so too had it brought mechanisation to all aspects of tea-growing. Tea was very well adapted to the tropical north, and agronomically there were few problems. In the huge state of Queensland, there was more than enough suitable land to produce the country's entire tea requirements, and Australians were recognised tea addicts.

Guy, as an astute businessman as well as a major grower, was marketing his own product and apparently enjoying phenomenal success, but overall, Trenton Estates were committed to continually upgrading quality more than obtaining the greatest possible profit. A good deal of capital was tied up in the all-important manufacturing process.

'Harvesting this morning,' Guy told her at breakfast. 'Coming?'

'Try and stop me.' Sara, who had been slicing a ripe, golden mango, looked up and gave him a brilliant smile.

'Pity we couldn't get that cast off sooner,' Guy observed. 'We could make good use of you.'

He made her wear a huge, almond-green coolie hat that sat charmingly on her rich, glowing hair and played up the depth of green in her eyes. It was very hot in the fields but scenically very beautiful. The sky was invariably a deep perfect turquoise, the ranges that rose out of the luxuriant green tropical rain-forest purple at their crown. Up and down the slopes in neat rows were the glossy, thriving tea bushes and protecting the perimeter of the property and beautifying the grounds were the fabulous decorative trees of the north.

Sara found the progress of the harvester, sitting astride and atop the compact rows, quite fascinating.

'This requires the most skill and precision of all field operations,' Guy told her. 'Sure it's not too hot for you?' He lifted a damp red-gold curl from her cheek.

'I don't even notice it.'

'No, you don't.' He gave her his devastating, sidelong smile. 'It's a little extraordinary for a redhead but on no account remove that hat from your head.'

'I've had no problems to date. I'm lucky. My skin doesn't freckle or burn.'

His jewelled glance touched her face, lingering on her creamy skin. 'Nevertheless I don't want to have to deal with sunstroke. It can be very unpleasant.'

'Yes, Guy.' She sighed sweetly. 'What about the variation in the slope?' she asked intelligently. 'How does the harvester cope?'

'A good question. The upper limit of the slope is set by the ability of the harvester to pluck the tea in that area. Adjustments are made on the plucking-head and the rows are plucked in *exactly* the same way at each harvest. The effect of the slope on the plucking-height doesn't then vary. Poor harvesting, needless to say, limits the yield and affects the quality of the manufactured tea.'

'What about pests and diseases?' Sara raised her green eyes to his striking profile.

'We're easily able to deal with them through chemical and cultural control. The land here is really ideal for tea-growing. We're going to build a great industry, Sara. Tea is a crop which has an economic life of fifty years and more. Many of the tea plantations in India and Sri Lanka are over a hundred years old and still in production. My family planned this plantation very thoroughly and carefully made use of all their experience in Sri Lanka. It's extremely difficult to correct mistakes as a plantation develops. We've got a set-up here that's very nearly perfect.

Yields and quality are high. I'm going to make it the best there is.'

'I've no doubt of that!' Sara acknowledged the intensely male drive. 'What about cyclones?'

He looked away across the brilliant green valley. 'Tea bushes are very compact and strong. We've been deluged. We've had hail. But, disallowing something like Cyclone Tracy that devastated Darwin, monsoonal storms aren't all that much of a problem. Unless they blow the factory over.'

'*What?*'

'Joking!' His lean fingers gently pinched her chin. 'We've built to be cyclone-proof.'

'You, your father: both of you very progressive men. You must have been very proud of him? *My* father...' A little expression of pain crossed her face.

'Go on.'

Sara thrust her hands deep into the patch pockets of her skirt. 'I don't usually talk about him. I feel it's not very nice...disloyal.'

'You're talking to me, Sara,' he pointed out quietly. 'You know I respect your confidences, and sometimes conflicts have to be talked out. Maybe we can't always solve them, but we can try to *understand*.'

'I suppose so.' Her little smile was bitter-sweet. 'I trust you, Guy. That's not easy for me. I grew up in a state of struggle. I've had everything, then again, I've missed out on a lot. Or I think I have. It's the same thing. Because my father was the male in my life and his control was so oppressive, perhaps my attitudes have become a bit extreme. It had almost come to the point where a dynamic kind of man like yourself symbolised all I had come to dislike and fear. I was reared to believe man was the measure of the human race. Women are valued only for their beauty. They cannot contribute anything significant. I've been fighting *that* all my life. I did very well at school and university, yet my father was never interested in my achievements, only in so far as I didn't disgrace him. I made the quota to read law, yet my ambitions were treated with amused contempt. My father saw no point at all in my making the effort to gain a law degree. Even if I did, he assured me, like most women I would reject a career for marriage.'

'The assumption being you couldn't have both?'

'I *do* want marriage, Guy, if I could ever trust a man. Love, marriage, children. I'll certainly permit *my* children free thought.'

'But surely you're young enough to pursue your dreams? Is it money?'

'I could manage. *Now*. I couldn't then. My father is a wealthy man. That doesn't mean he handed it around. The only way of life I was offered was one that pleased him. As long as I did that Mummy and I didn't have a hard time. I could have defined my independence earlier, but it seemed to me Mummy needed me. Goodness knows I was wrong. My parents actually get on a whole lot better when I'm not around.'

'That's sad, Sara!' was his instinctive response. 'Your mother is a lovely woman and you're certainly not lacking in love and affection there, but you must see she's no rebel. Her temperament would allow her to bow more easily to your father's wishes, and she does love him, Sara, for all his extremes. No one, not even you, can get inside your parents' marriage. Perhaps in a sense your father found *you* a threat. He impressed me as a clever, ice-cool man, but that doesn't mean he's particularly mature in his personal relationships. Maybe he couldn't handle being a father. His break-off point was being a husband. Parenting doesn't come with the ability to have children. Your father wanted you to conform so that he could dominate you. You refused to be dominated. You turned away from each other. I don't know what the solution is. I *do* know you can't continue to hold up your father as the male model. Surely you can see the dangers in that? Your initial response to me was aggression. It was emotional and it related to your father.'

'I know that!' She threw up her head and her green eyes sparkled. 'But knowing things doesn't always help us cope with them better.'

'So you're going to continue to hate me just a little?'

'I'm sure it's a whole lot safer. I've seen how a woman's capacity for loving can be turned against her.'

'So the bottom line is domination. Passion is emotional domination, is that it? You don't want a man who's going to make you *feel*? I suppose that explains Palmer, to some extent.'

They returned home for lunch, and afterwards went down to the factory to see the green leaf carried by conveyor from one manufacturing process to the next. Because biochemical and physical changes took place immediately the green leaf was plucked, the harvest was not stored in the field but taken within a few hours to the factory. Even in transit the plucked leaf was loosely packed to permit free air movement.

'You'll be able to see everything if I sit you up here,' Guy said, lifting her by the waist up on to a high bench.

'This is fine.'

A smile touched his mouth. 'You can't fade into the background. Titian hair. Yellow dress.'

She had to struggle not to lean forward and clasp her arms around his neck.

'Briefly what happens is this,' he said, mercifully missing her warm look. 'The tea is withered and loses water. Next it's crushed, torn and cut. Fermented, then dried to stop the chemical and biochemical changes, after which it's graded with different-sized sieves and all fibre and stalk removed. The crushing, tearing, cutting-machine you see there, the CTC, is called the rotovane. Anything else you want to know I'll be happy to explain. I want to talk to Tom for a few minutes. There are so many fine points that have to be worked out. OK?'

She touched her creamy temple in a salute.

Several of the workers, in fact, came up to her to say hello and answer her questions. She was welcomed wherever she went, and it was obvious the staff approved of her interest. For their part all Guy's people were tremendously *involved*. His authority was absolute but completely unforced. If any man had the unselfconscious habit of command, he did. Sara didn't realise her green glance was almost hungry, but Guy, casually checking back on her, broke off what he was doing rather abruptly.

'What was the meaning of that very intense glance?'

'I can see I'll have to guard my expression.'

'Answer the question.' He looked straight into her eyes.

'Why is it so important for you to know?'

'I have strong feelings for you, Sara.'

'One hopes, *friendly*?' The taunt was a bit shaky.

'You're an evasive little witch.'

'I've been taught to suppress my feelings and cover up.'

'Do you feel guilty because your body craves mine?'

'I give up!' she cried passionately. 'All I was thinking about was *tea*.'

'I'm sure your mother didn't encourage you to tell lies. Tea couldn't have been further from your mind. You stopped me in my tracks.'

'That doesn't sound like you,' she jeered sweetly. 'I thought you impervious to a woman's glance.'

'You like taking risks, don't you?'

The expression in his eyes made her heart race.

'Are there any tigers in Sri Lanka?'

'Not as house-guests.'

'I never cease to be amazed by your golden eyes. In your own way you're a very handsome, dangerous creature.'

'Then you ought to show me the proper respect.'

Tom Reed, the manager, cut short the gentle intensity of their exchange. He called to Guy and Guy adjusted his expression, straightened up and moved off.

And how, Sara wondered, is he going to react when I tell him I've been invited over to Wayne's tonight?

She mentioned it as he was taking her back to the house.

'What was that? I can't hear you.'

'I hate you when you're mean. Will you take me or shall I ask him to call?'

'You *want* to talk to Wayne?' He slanted a brilliant glance at her.

'He's already started on the preliminary sketches for my portrait.'

'What do you do when he's sketching, drop off?'

'We *talk*.'

'He seems to be blooming under your indulgent regard.'

'Yes, we're getting very close.'

'Val is obviously of the belief you're going to take over where she leaves off.'

'Hey now, it's not like that!' Sara's eyelids were drooping but she sat up very quickly.

'Oh, my dear, but it *is*. I have eyes. Val has been on the look-out for her replacement. She wants to retire and she has an instinct for women with causes. Neither of you has had an easy time and, best of all, you have the competence to push Wayne to his limits.'

'This is all in your head, Guy!' She gave an agonised little moan.

'I think not.' His brilliant eyes held mockery and concern both.

'Can't you trust me to be sensible? *Please,* Cousin Guy?'

His eyes glittered at her beguiling expression. 'I'm not inclined to laugh.'

'Isn't there *anything* I can do to please you?'

'Sure,' he returned tersely. 'Make up your mind where you want to be.'

In the cool of late afternoon Sara joined Clare in the garden. Armed with secateurs, Clare was cutting masses of bird of paradise flowers for one of her arrangements. Sara wheeled her chair alongside, confirming the sense of warmth and closeness she felt towards Guy's aunt. They were laughing quietly about something when suddenly Clare broke off as a silver station-wagon swept up the drive.

'Goodness!' Clare gasped.

'Something wrong?'

Clare met her look with a little frown. 'Nothing, dear. Nothing at all. I expect I'm surprised. It's a neighbour of ours, Annabel Stacey. She and her brother should have been away for months.'

Annabel! Now Clare had Sara's full attention. Jake had mentioned an Annabel.

'You don't sound much as though you like her.'

'My dear, it won't take you two minutes to find out. She has a thing about Guy.'

'Really?' A long moment passed. 'And how does Guy feel about this?'

'I wouldn't dream of asking him.' Clare placed the last flower-head in her basket. 'Of course, she's heard you're here.'

'Do you mean I'm being checked out?'

'I dare say. Don't lose any sleep about it.'

Sara had never felt more conscious of her broken leg as their visitor dashed nimbly up the slope. 'Hi, there,' she called. 'I couldn't wait for an invitation to meet your guest.'

'What did I tell you?' Clare whispered, then went forward very graciously. 'Annabel, dear, we had no idea you had returned. Surely you intended to be away for months?'

'Old Clive got restless!' Annabel laughingly explained but her startling blue gaze was trained on Sara's face.

'Allow me to introduce you,' Clare said.

Sara felt she had never before been subjected to such a thorough scrutiny. Even the roots of her hair.

'I was told you were very beautiful and you *are*. I don't think I've seen such glorious hair. Must be an awful problem in the sun though?'

'Actually, no,' Sara smiled.

Clare invited Annabel up to the house and Annabel got behind Sara's wheelchair, grasping it very purposefully. 'It must be terrible for you confined to this thing.'

'I'll be glad to be out of it.'

'Still, being helpless must have its advantages.'

'Name one,' Sara challenged, giving their visitor a curious look.

'Goodness, does being incapacitated make you cross?'

'Not at all. I was giving some thought to your question.'

Esther brought them afternoon tea out on the veranda, and scarcely had Annabel put the cup to her lips than Sara once more came into the firing-line.

'Won't you tell me about your experiences in the jungle?' she begged.

'You didn't read about them?'

'Actually I did, but it's not the same as hearing first hand. My God, weren't you lucky to have Guy! I suppose you fell in love with him.'

'Of course!' Sara sighed voluptuously. 'He's the most incredible man.'

Clare took a large swallow of her tea. 'Speaking of Guy, does he know you're home?'

Annabel's blue eyes held an odd flicker. 'It's going to be such a joy to surprise him. We weren't contacted until it was all over, otherwise I'd have been here. I would have been out of my mind had I known. To lose *Guy*!' She swept an agitated hand through the short wing of white-blonde hair that fell forward on her tanned forehead.

'They were terrible days,' Clare agreed, 'but thank God everyone survived.'

Annabel responded with a racking sigh.

'And how is Clive?' Clare decided to get on to something more cheerful.

'Really he's so severe these days. Not a bit of fun.'

'I expect he worries about you, Annabel,' Clare supplied.

'Whatever for?' Annabel opened wide her strange, light eyes. 'Look what I've become. A farmer. I mean I actually live and work on a *farm*!'

'That doesn't please you?' Sara asked.

'It puts me in a rage!' Annabel gave Sara a brittle, brilliant smile. 'I lost my husband two years ago and afterwards I had a breakdown. I simply couldn't cope with my grief.'

'I'm so sorry.' Sara was moved to quick sympathy.

'Dear old Clive came to my rescue. He brought me back to the farm. To my true friends. Guy—you too, Clare—have been such tremendous support.'

'So what was her husband like?' Sara asked Clare some forty fraught minutes later.

'As different from Guy as it's possible for a man to be.'

'You mean she didn't love him?' Incredulously Sara shook her head.

'There are only two people in the world Annabel loves,' Clare sighed. 'Herself and Guy.'

Another door swung wide.

They got very little reaction out of Guy.

'Annabel and Clive are back.' Clare stared at him over the top of the flowers.

'But they just left!' Gratefully he accepted a long, cold drink from Sara's hand.

'She said she wanted to surprise you,' Sara supplied innocently.

'Is there a certain roguishness in your tone?'

'A woman like that would keep things rippling.'

'My dear Sara,' he said drily, 'I'm wholly immune.'

'I'm looking forward to seeing that borne out in the days ahead.'

'Shouldn't you be dressing for the Palmers?' he countered.

'I've a perfectly super sari laid out.'

'Surely not the green and gold?'

She had been going well until he looked at her, then a delicious flush graced her skin. She would always connect that exquisite garment with Guy and no one else.

'Everything OK with Guy?' Wayne asked her after Guy had dropped her off. 'He looked as if he doesn't trust you out of his sight.'

'One can scarcely credit he'd turn into a mother hen.'

'I've heard old Annabel's back,' Wayne supplied almost gleefully. 'Of course you know she's always been in love with him.'

'I should think she'd be duty bound. Everyone knows how good he is at moral support.'

Both Wayne and Val were heavily into gossip, so Sara heard a great deal during the space of the evening. Val, in a brilliant hand-painted cotton mumu, was a tiny woman, barely five feet, but her presence was twice as tall.

'Of course she's appropriating her brother's life! Eventually he'll come to realise what a fool he's been. He gave up a lovely woman for Annabel. The two didn't get on.'

'Her sole concern has always been Guy,' Wayne pointed out. 'I believe she used to keep a photograph of him on her dressing-table even when she was married.'

Sara gave a horrified laugh.

Dinner was delicious. Val was a superb cook and Wayne supplied the wine, a fine Chardonnay. They worked their way through oysters Kilpatrick, succulent white fish fillets done in a piquant prawn sauce and pineapple Marsala.

Sara complimented Val sincerely and Val beamed her pleasure. 'It's lovely to serve a meal to an appreciative guest!'

Sara could see that in Val's eyes she fell little short of perfect. It was worrying, because all she could give of herself was a sincere friendship, hardly a life of service.

'No one ever did find out what went wrong between Guy and that girl.' Mother and son exchanged a deep look. 'There's no denying she's a striking-looking creature. She's not a natural blonde at all but still, it's extremely effective. I'm not against hair colour. I do it myself. But those *eyes*! Not normal if you ask me. What did you think of her, Sara?'

'She seemed very tense. Very highly strung. Of course she *did* lose her husband. She may have some little obsession about Guy, but I can't believe she'd get into marriage without caring about the person she married.'

Mother and son snorted. Both of them were at pains to suggest that a bond existed between Guy and Annabel all but impossible to break.

As an evening it weighed in as more upsetting than entertaining. Val's incessant hints settled like a heavy cloud.

She kissed Sara goodnight; the sort of kiss only a prospective daughter-in-law in the state of grace could expect to receive. 'That plaster comes off next week, doesn't it?'

'Oh, I hope so!' Sara breathed fervently. One had to be absolutely in the pink to cope with Val and Wayne.

'We're keen to have you with us,' Val told her fondly. 'We did ask *first*.'

'Mamma rather dotes on you,' Wayne told her when Sara was comfortably settled in his car. 'You've been wonderful for us both.'

'That's kind of you, Wayne,' Sara answered a little helplessly, 'but I've really done very little.'

'As it happens, that's not true. You're only being modest. Most girls I've known, Leigh for example, have clashed with Mamma, but she approves of you unreservedly.'

It was a heavy burden to carry.

They were half-way back to the plantation when Wayne's car came to a spluttering halt.

'My God, no!' he cried and gave Sara an embarrassed glance.

'Out of petrol?' she responded levelly.

'Well, Val did go out this morning, but the gauge says enough. Don't worry, I'll find out.' He stepped out with deceptive purpose. He had never been one to ascertain quickly what went wrong with his car.

Fifty minutes later and they were still beached on the side of the road. Wayne had been kept busy tinkering and making trips to and fro to propose this and that to Sara.

'I don't suppose you'd be too keen to spend the night here,' he asked doubtfully.

'You *can't* get it going?' Sara felt a great thrill of irritation.

'Obviously not.' Wayne exuded a general air of apology, but not worry. 'I never was much good at mechanical things. What's the time?'

'Little short of midnight.'

'Late for us,' he observed. 'Probably Val is getting worried. She never settles until I get in.'

'She seems like a devoted mother.'

'Guy might come looking for us,' Wayne then reasoned. 'He wasn't too happy about my driving you home as it was.'

Sara looked up at the glittering canopy of stars. 'Even if you could walk back I wouldn't care to stay here by myself. Country roads are very lonely.'

'Someone *might* come along,' Wayne murmured. 'In fact, I hope they don't. It's marvellous to have you all to myself. Sara?' Wayne slipped into the car beside her.

'*Please,* Wayne.'

'You never allow me to make love to you.'

'I like you, Wayne. I admire your work, but you have a problem if you're expecting a love affair.'

'I know what it is,' Wayne said solicitously. 'That damned plaster on your leg. I expect it feels ten times the weight.'

'It's a nuisance, I know that.'

'You're getting angry.' He leaned over and kissed her cheek. 'Poor Sara is tired. Why don't you put your head on my shoulder? We can see the dawn in together. Val said you're a girl who won't be rushed. She shares your values.'

Sara saw the headlights before he did. Wayne had his eyes shut, murmuring quietly.

'Someone coming!'

Wayne tried to sound pleased. 'Good. I think it's probably the Wilsons.' He swung his head towards the rear. 'Now I'm in the stew!' he muttered bleakly. 'Even money it's the Merc?'

'When you have a lot of people depending on you, you need a dependable car.'

Guy parked the Mercedes directly opposite and crossed the road. 'You might consider everyone was worried.'

Sara, who was faint with relief to see him, didn't show it at all. 'What's actually wrong with getting home after midnight?'

'As far as *I'm* concerned, Sara,' he told her coolly, 'you don't have to call me to check in. *Val* was anxious.'

'God, you'd think I was a small boy!' Wayne burst out petulantly.

'If it comes to that, what *are* you doing? Is this your notion of a secluded spot?'

The shameless mockery of his tone made Sara's eyes flash. 'I just hope the Mercedes breaks down one day very soon.'

'I'm bound to know what to do about it, Sara. Besides being a tea-planter I'm also an engineer.'

'There's a legend going around there's nothing you can't do.'

'What's the trouble, Wayne?' Guy ignored her.

'If he knew, would we be sitting here?'

'It could be anything,' Wayne volunteered. 'I'm absolutely no mechanic.'

'I'd better take a look, then,' Guy said briskly and went back to the Mercedes to get a high-powered flashlight.

'I suppose I'd better get out,' Wayne said indecisively.

'There's the chance you might learn something.'

Inside two minutes Guy had the engine running.

'What was it?' Sara asked.

'Haven't the foggiest notion!' Wayne laughed. 'I'll lift you into Guy's car, shall I?'

'I've got these beastly sticks.'

There was a faint sob in her voice and Guy moved quickly, ever the man of action. 'Open the door, Wayne, if you don't mind.'

Wayne rushed to be helpful.

On the way back to the plantation Sara began to giggle tiredly.

'What's the joke?'

'I can't do a *thing* all by myself.'

'You mean you couldn't get away from Palmer?'

'Wayne was a perfect gentleman. Which is more than I can say for you.'

'And what is that, a flash of ancient, bitter resentment? I think you'd better accept that you can't insult me and pull it off.'

'Yet it is quite acceptable for you to imply I was indulging in some feverish necking.'

'That's perhaps carrying it a bit far. I'm sure Wayne can manoeuvre his way around a romantic interlude. He was quietly seething when I arrived.'

'Wayne was no problem at all.'

'Then he must have phenomenal self-control.'

She glanced at him sideways; this man with the arrogant air of a tiger. 'Aren't you going rather fast?'

'I know the road.'

'And of course you've bought off the police.' She was still fighting authority figures, the more vigorously because this one she *loved*. What did it matter if she admitted it to herself?

Something in her tone prompted him to look at her quickly. 'How many glasses of wine did you have?'

'I wish I knew!' She shrugged the question off. 'I certainly ate and drank everything Val put before me. Did she really ring?'

'We keep in regular contact. Has something upset you?'

'I do feel under a mild strain.'

'Maybe Wayne and Val are attempting to pressure you. I know from past experience that they work as a team. You can't get pushed into a role you haven't chosen.'

'I can take care of it,' she said. 'You're the one who isn't what he pretends to be.'

'You have some weird notions firmly entrenched in your mind. It's a pity because basically it's a fine, receptive mind.'

'Only I'm not as worldly as you.'

'You seem to be eager for a fight. May I know why?'

'Maybe I'm angry I've played into your hands. You dissolve all my doubts, then fresh ones spring up.'

'Does this have anything to do with meeting Annabel Stacey?' he asked with striking crispness.

'Ah, your ex-girlfriend!'

'I seem to recall you thought Leigh was my girlfriend.'

'Don't all men consider half a dozen relationships as their right?'

'You seem to have formed a few in the short time I've known you.'

'Did Annabel really marry another man when she loved you?'

'So that's it,' he said tersely. 'You've had a nice social evening dredging up the past.'

'In fact we only mentioned you now and again.'

'So why do you want to cry?'

'I *don't*!' She was shaken that he knew.

'It's just the sort of thing the Palmers would do. Wayne's as much an old gossip as his mother.'

'In any case it's none of *my* business.'

He replied by running the big car off the road.

'Guy?'

'Don't panic, Sara. We've made up ten minutes. Clare won't know.'

'Take me home,' she said shakily. 'I don't want to talk.'

'Neither do I.' His hand slid into her hair 'Making love to you is the only way I can get you to be yourself.'

His jewelled eyes flashed, and as she looked up at him in a kind of yearning agony he lowered his head with faint violence and caught up her thirsting lips.

She was lost immediately. All she could think of was the love that raged in her. She was whimpering with the force of it, her shoulder trembling with his grip.

'I'm going to have you, Sara. Sure as I live!' he grated. He buried his face in the curve of her neck, turned up her chin, ran his mouth down the creamy column of her throat to the pulse that beat in agitation in the soft hollow at its base. 'Little idiot! Annabel is nothing!'

She let out a long fluttery breath, folding towards him like a flower. 'You don't tell me what *I* am.'

'You're a little witch who doesn't understand her own power.'

He kissed her until she saw dizzying patterns behind her eyes, and when she was ready to crumple he put her away from him. He was breathing fast and it was obvious the forces within him hadn't found physical release.

'I can't take much more of this!' he flashed with curbed violence. 'Loving you properly would accomplish more than I could ever *say*. The day you get that plaster off can't come soon enough.'

CHAPTER EIGHT

SARA sat up on the table and the doctor bent over her frail-looking white leg.

'You've mended beautifully. Good girl.'

Sister offered congratulations.

'Do you want to lie down for a moment, Sara?' Guy suggested. 'You've gone very white.'

'So she has!' Doctor Morrison looked at her keenly. 'You've been really worrying, haven't you?'

'It's not unheard of to go back into plaster.'

'You've mended splendidly as I said.'

Guy, too, from being uncharacteristically rattled, showed a wave of relief. 'Lunch,' he decided. 'You look as though you need a seven-course meal. You're as fragile as a paper doll.'

There were several restaurants to choose from but as fate would have it they had to pick the one Annabel and her brother Clive had decided on after a long morning in the town.

Sara was betrayed into a little dismayed sound and Guy, who had been reading the menu, looked around swiftly.

'So this is where you eat when you come to town!' Annabel made directly for them, embracing Guy's wide shoulders. 'Clive, dear, you don't know Sara, do you? Guy's house-guest.'

The head waiter hovered uncertainly but there was embarrassment in Clive Chadwick's rather fine grey eyes.

The two men were greeting each other, shaking hands.

'Plaster off, Sara? You must be terrifically pleased.' Annabel moved so that she had a good view of Sara's legs. 'Oooh, my dear, how *thin* you've become!'

'It will be a different story in a couple of weeks. Guy has engaged a physiotherapist for me.'

Annabel's finely cut nostrils flared but she kept smiling. 'Oh, do let's all eat together!'

'I don't think...' Clive Chadwick met Sara's eyes wryly and, sensible to his quick flush, Sara smiled and gestured.

'Why not?'

'Oh, this is lovely!' Annabel confirmed gaily. 'We have so much to talk about.'

In fact she dominated the talk during lunch but, far from being laboured, her wit made them all laugh. At her best she was a very attractive, scintillating woman. The sun shone dully on her smooth ash-blonde hair. She was wearing a very chic sleeveless V-necked dress in red with large black dots and her glamour triumphed over the intensity of the colour.

She flirted with Guy in a long-practised manner, making much of her eyes and brilliant smiles. He fended off her little sallies with a quick, dry humour and it was fairly obvious that under the right circumstances he found her good company. Clive was much quieter but he impressed with his essential *niceness* and good sense.

'How long will you be staying on now, Sara?' Annabel finally asked over coffee. 'We can't allow you to go home without seeing our place. It's not the Taj Mahal,' she directed a smiling glance at Guy, 'but we've put lots of work into it.'

Sara evaded the question by asking after their tropical fruit farm.

Clive smiled at her and launched into a hymn of praise of the rural life. 'Of course fruit is terribly susceptible to storm damage, as you can imagine. Not like tea, it can survive anything! Our mangoes are ruined if it's wet when the trees are in flower, and we've had a whole crop of pawpaws and avocados wiped out.'

They parted company with Sara rather forced into the promise to visit the farm.

'What did you think of Clive?' Guy asked.

'A nice man. A teeny bit tedious when he gets on to his favourite subject.'

'Which happens to be fruit. You were very good about it all. Annabel thinks nothing of crashing in on somebody else's party.'

'Despite that, she was quite amusing.'

'Hmm.' He looked a little thoughtful. 'Some demon drives her. Poor Annabel, she hasn't been terribly adroit with her life. How are you feeling?' His golden eyes blazed all over her face.

'A bit cautious with my leg. Otherwise, fine. You've been very gentle with me this morning.'

'It's impossible not to be.' He put a protective arm around her, and for a moment Sara allowed herself to lean against him, a breathless soft weight. 'Let's take the long way home,' he murmured. 'I'm wild to take you in my arms.'

Every inch of her skin registered his nearness. In an elemental way she fed on his abundant strength. His radiant physicalness was an important part of his persona, a pleasure-force that was dazzling.

'Sara?' He could feel the trembling in her body.

'I can't think of anything I want more.'

A quick return to mobility meant great freedom for Sara. It was almost as though Guy had presented her with wings. She roamed everywhere over the estate and the magnificent verdant countryside, and it seemed to her that this was the right place to make an excellent documentary.

'I have been asked before,' Guy told her, laughing a little at her excitement.

'The tea-gardens are so beautiful and the plantation house is magnificent. Surely a feature film could only do good. Can't I persuade you?'

'What form will it take?' His golden eyes challenged her.

'How about a hug?'

'That will do for a start. You surely can't mean Kirkman's company?'

'I wish I could think of someone else. But Evan's the best.'

'I seem to recall his inappropriate behaviour made you forfeit your job.'

'So it did!' Sara looked and sounded surprised. 'Which just goes to show what sort of impression Evan made on me. What I want to do now is show the excellence of Trenton Estates. Please say you'll give your permission.'

'I'll do that when I get a guarantee from Kirkman that he knows how to behave!' Guy returned crisply.

Evan's behaviour over the three days of shooting was impeccable, but when a celebration party was held on the Saturday night, all his pious promises took wing. Alcohol played a significant part in sweeping away good sense, but Sara's appearance that night was the *coup de grâce*. She wore green, her favourite colour; a brilliant, water-lily green in Thai silk.

'Didn't that fool get the message?' Guy asked her tersely. 'Tell him to cool it, or *I* will.'

'You have no confidence in me at all!' she retorted and tilted her chin.

Even Wayne was annoyed and plainly censorious. 'I understood Kirkman was *married*?'

'Oh he *is*!' Sara confirmed with a flash of her green eyes. 'But he's got some idea it shouldn't prevent him from having a good time.'

'I feel like popping him one,' Wayne said belligerently. 'You haven't seen Leigh, by the way, have you?

She called at the house during the week but I missed her. I wonder what she wanted.'

'Why don't you ask her? She hasn't got her father with her.'

For the rest of the night Sara was like a cat on hot bricks. Keeping away from Evan kept her perpetually on the move but eventually he caught up with her, grasping her around the waist and dancing her out on to a secluded end of the enveloping veranda.

'Sara, Sara, you look gorgeous.'

'I know. You've told me. At least a dozen times. You've told everyone within earshot. All of them know you have a wife at home.'

'I haven't seen her for more than a week.'

'Does that mean you've forgotten what she looks like? Try and behave yourself, Evan. The condition on which your company was allowed up here was you got yourself straightened out.'

'Well...' Evan turned down his mouth humorously. 'I can't suppress one last little fling.' He grabbed her hand and pressed it to his lips. 'Have you got Trenton on the hook too?'

'I won't stop him from laying you out on the grass.'

'He could do it, too.'

'Then shall we go in?'

'He'd only hit me 'cause I'm short. Wouldn't you feel sorry for me, Sara, if I had a bleeding nose?'

'Not at all.'

'You're a cold little bitch!' He wagged a finger at her. 'I've missed you. God, I've missed you. The entire crew miss you. We used to pause every day in remembrance.'

Sara tossed her long hair back over her shoulder. 'I swear I missed you all too in a way. Sometimes, in the evenings when the programme comes on. Please, Evan, do the right thing. Guy is looking daggers at me.'

'I wouldn't be too frightened,' Evan drawled with extreme deliberation, 'you're his little white lamb.'

'Red's more my shade. Come on, let's go in.'

'I want a kiss. Just one.' He put out his arm and tugged her towards him.

'Are you perfectly crazy?'

Evan appeared to reflect. 'No, I don't think so. You have the most b-b-bootiful mouth. It's so soft and full. Let's hop over the rails and head for the woods.'

'It's more interesting inside.'

'Hello, hello, now *who's* having fun?'

'Aren't you the witty one!' Evan spun around as Annabel came towards them with a malicious little laugh. 'I was just about to kiss Sara only you came out to spoil it all.'

'But Mr Kirkman, aren't you a married man?'

'I'm a long way from home.'

Sara could feel the embarrassed heat under her skin. 'Shall we all go in?'

Annabel, in striking black and white, eyed her appreciatively. 'You're quite a girl, do you know? That patrician little air is a great cover. What *are* you anyway, and what are you doing here?'

'And how is that *your* business?' Evan was positively on Sara's side. 'You're just jealous because Sara's captured the attention of your old friend.'

'He's a lot more than that,' Annabel returned with a contemptuous face. 'You television people don't know how to behave, do you?'

'Oh, I like that!' Evan crowed. 'When you've been playing the harlot all night.'

Sara gasped, frozen in her tracks, but Annabel teetered forward a few steps and caught Evan's cheek with a flying hand. 'You bastard, how *dare* you?' She was seething, *seething*, her pale, pale eyes like chunks of ice.

'Oh, you *naughty* girl!' Evan, backing off, gave a startled cry.

'It wouldn't be the first time you've had your face smacked.'

'Do you think so? It *is*.' Almost sober, Evan began to massage his cheek. 'You've got a super right.'

'I demand an apology,' Annabel gritted.

'D-d-don't, dear. You won't get one.'

'All right then.' Annabel appeared to look around for something to throw.

'Annabel, *please*,' Sara pleaded.

'The reason you're still on the shelf, dear, is you've got a murderous temper.' Evan put his arms around Sara and stood her in front of him.

'Boy, is this one of the marks of a coward!' Sara tried to unlock his grasp, her hair tumbling forward when a hard, cutting voice addressed them all from the french doors.

'I'd advise you all to cut it out. *Now*.'

'Oh, *Guy*!' Annabel's blazing eyes incredibly misted over. She made a little rush at him and started to cling to his arm. 'I want you to order this man off.'

'Which *man*?' Guy asked. His striking-looking face was a mask of contempt.

'Me, of course.' Evan gave a little bow. 'Sorry about that, old chap. Swear I won't do it again.'

'Do you know what he called me?' Annabel broke in. 'A *harlot*.'

'So you are. Almost.'

'Oh, *Evan*.' Sara closed her eyes for a moment, then grasped Evan's arm. 'Do stop. If you can.'

'Boys will be boys, love.'

'And girls will be girls. You apologise to Annabel and she'll apologise to you.'

'That's a *leetle* bit difficult!'

'Perhaps you'd like to call it a night,' Guy suggested caustically. 'I'll get someone to run you back into town.'

'Oh, I say, that's kind of you.'

'It is,' Guy responded, very quietly.

'I do mean that.' Evan lowered his eyes. There was rather more of Trenton than he cared to chew.

'Perhaps Sara could tell us why she's having an affair with a married man,' Annabel persisted stubbornly. 'She's the one who ought to be called a harlot.'

'You apologise for that or I'll pull your hair,' Evan warned her.

'I came out on to the veranda and they were *kissing*.'

'Goodness, you're a liar as well,' Evan accused her. 'I'll take an oath on a stack of Bibles that I failed.'

'It would be rather nice to believe you,' Guy said crisply. 'I don't think we should continue the conversation now. My guests might think it strange if we *all* started to act rather badly. Kirkman, I'll walk you down to my car. Sara,' he said very coolly, 'will you tell Tom to collect the keys and drive Mr Kirkman back to his hotel?'

'But surely you should *throw* him out!' Annabel cried violently.

'I don't think so. The main reason being he won't be invited any more, and it's sure to create a scene.' He moved towards Evan and gestured with his hand. 'Shall we?'

'I know I've behaved a bit stupidly,' Evan said. 'Apart from that, I've enjoyed myself immensely.'

'It's right. And right again,' Guy advised.

'So it's off I go!' Evan turned back and saluted Sara with his hand. ''Bye, gorgeous. I'll remember you all my life.'

'A week would be too long.' Sara shook her head. 'Tell me I'm forgiven.'

'You're forgiven, Evan.' Her expression was a mixture of wry humour and utter seriousness.

'If you asked me I'd fight Trenton here.' Guy put a hand on his shoulder and Evan called, 'Maybe not. Don't let the terrible Annabel take it out on you.'

'I thought you were *going*, Sara?' Guy clipped out.

Reaction flooded her. 'Yes, Mr Trenton,' she returned smartly. 'Certainly, sir. I'll do it immediately.'

'Did she ever tell you about her domineering old father?' Evan asked.

Less than an hour later, all their guests had gone home. 'I'd call that a great success, wouldn't you?' Clare took her beautiful diamond earrings off and set them down on a sofa table. 'I don't even feel like going to bed.'

Sara bent over and kissed her cheek. 'If it was a great success, much of it is due to you. You're a wonderful hostess.'

'Thank you, dear.' Clare patted her hand. 'What was that little business later on? Annabel followed you with a face like one of the avenging furies.'

'Evan was a bit silly, that's all.'

'I thought he was rather funny,' Clare smiled. 'One couldn't help wishing, however, that he would take his marriage vows seriously. He must give his wife a terrible time.'

'Evan is notorious for chasing women,' Sara said. 'I'm convinced it's a basic lack of self-esteem. The more emotionally retarded a man is, the more he tries to bed every woman in sight. It's a shame, because he *is* likeable, and he's very good at his job. The documentary will be a great success.'

'And more publicity for the plantation!' Clare put her soft dark head back and gave a stifled yawn. 'So what made Annabel so bitter?'

'Believe it or not, Evan called her a harlot.'

'A *what*?' Clare sat up, round-eyed.

'Oh, they say it all the time these days,' Sara explained. 'Mummy reacts just like you. My generation are very free with ugly words. She was very angry. She slapped his face. It was quite a blow.'

'For goodness' sake!' Clare was amazed. 'And how did it come about?'

'Good question, Clare,' Guy observed smoothly, coming back into the drawing-room after seeing to all the lighting.

'I don't think we should bother with all that now,' Sara said coolly. 'The whole thing was absurd.'

'What a nerve!' Guy lifted a black eyebrow.

Clare flickered a perceptive glance at them. 'Ah well, I'd better go to bed if I want to be fresh in the morning.'

'I'll come too,' Sara said hurriedly.

'You needn't think I'm going to shut up the house alone,' Guy told her coolly. 'You asked for a party.'

'I did *not*!'

'You have very speaking *eyes*. Now you help me shut up.'

'Don't be too long,' Clare smiled. She went to Guy and he bent his dark head and brushed her cheek. 'I thought Sara and I might go over to the Reef next week.'

'I'll take you, of course.'

'*Could* you manage a few days?'

'Possibly—I don't know.'

'*See,* darling. 'Night, Sara.'

'You start this end, Sara,' Guy told her in a sleek voice after Clare had gone. 'I'll start the other.'

'You can be sure I won't be meeting you in the middle.'

'My dear, you don't have a snowball's chance in hell of getting away.'

That shook her. 'Your Annabel's the villain, not *me*!' She hardly meant to slam the door but she did.

'*My* Annabel doesn't have *your* dazzling sex-appeal.'

'You're just used to her, that's all. I thought she was pretty darn impressive tonight. Madonna would have found it difficult to upstage her.'

'And who's Madonna?' he asked in a perfectly serious voice.

'Is it possible you don't know?'

'Go on, tell me.'

'I thought she was in a class by herself, but the way Annabel comes on...'

'She wasn't toying with a married man.'

She was so angry she felt like attacking him with her long fingernails; instead she slammed another french door. *'Oh!'* She drew her hand back very quickly.

'Hoping I'll lose the thread?' Nevertheless he broke off what he was doing and moved towards her catching up the hand she was holding aloft. 'Hell, that's quite a splinter.'

'Get it out.'

'Really, Sara, have you forgotten how to say "please"?' He bent his dark head over hers. 'I think we need tweezers if we want to get it out in one piece.' He squeezed her finger slightly and she tried to catch the barely exposed top of the sliver of wood. 'That's no good. I recall seeing a pair of tweezers somewhere.'

'I know. In the garden-room. Clare used them when she caught a cactus needle down her nail.'

The night-blooming cereus was in breathtaking bloom, its flowers like enormous waxy cups encased in gold spikes. There was a dazzling array of blossoming plants in the garden-room with its great curved windows and earthy rattan furniture plushly upholstered, and, adorning the walls, two brilliant paintings of the Orientalist school. One of them filled Sara with endless fascination because the magnificent pasha astride a richly rugged and saddled white stallion was extraordinarily like Guy himself. It was a sumptuous painting, all luminous colour and soft, brilliant light, and she looked up at Guy and said drily, 'Sure you didn't pose for that?'

'What, in towering turban and brocaded robes? I wouldn't mind the horse. And the hunting leopard.'

'When I first saw you, you reminded me of something exotic, like the leopard. Someone terrible and dangerous, I thought.'

'Let's have a look at this splinter, shall we?'

He succeeded in removing it first time, and when a tiny little speck of blood welled, he lifted her hand and took her finger in his mouth.

She could have melted against him, so violently did he fire her blood. It was as if every vein in her body turned to high-voltage wires.

'Dracula!' she whispered softly, trying desperately to renounce the powerful temptations of the flesh.

'Shall we make it a blood pact?'

'What do I have to swear?'

'To tell the truth.' His golden, arrogant gaze struck her face. '*Were* you allowing Kirkman to kiss you?'

'Why is it you have such a poor image of me?'

'Why do you invariably answer a question with a question?'

Her odd little laugh was a bell in her throat. 'Do I ask *you* why you're reviving an affair with Annabel? She told us tonight you were much, much more than an old friend.'

'And they say *men* kiss and tell!' he drawled cynically.

'Is it worse for a woman to be promiscuous?'

'Much, much worse,' he returned curtly. 'And who the hell's promiscuous anyway?'

'You've slept with Annabel.'

'Do you want me to cite the lot?'

'Oh, you beast!' Her reaction was based on the force of her love for him. She had been struggling not to love him from the very first day.

Guy locked her two wrists in one grip. 'Stop it, Sara, I don't want to hurt you.'

'You damned well do!'

'You're so right!' He hauled her right into his arms. 'You're without any doubt the angriest female I've ever met. You're like some spitting little cat. You crave love and support but you've got it firmly entrenched in your mind it's got to be outright war. It's about time I retaliated.'

'Go on, do it then.' Her green eyes flashed. 'You're capable of anything. I know that. So I owe you a lot.'

'You don't owe me *anything*!' He swept her up like a doll.

'What are you going to do, rape me to death?'

'You'd hate being put over my knee even more.'

'You bet I would!' Her heart gave a great leap. 'I detest, absolutely *detest* the way men are so much stronger. You're all brutes and bullies. You're sub-human!'

He slumped hard on to a banquette with Sara in his arms. 'A little vixen like you would make any man a black-hearted tyrant. I joined the peace movement long ago. I thought I did. Until a flaming little rev-olutionary came along.'

'I'm happy when I'm left alone.'

'Are you?' He looked down into her flushed, ex-cited face and green, translucent eyes. 'You wouldn't mind being a slave for tonight.'

'Do I understand you? You want me to sleep with you?'

'My dear Sara,' he said caustically, 'I've never wanted anything else from the first day.'

'It's the only damned thing a man's honest about.'

'You don't want to sleep with me?' There was a brittle little smile around his shapely mouth.

'Perhaps I do,' she said fierily, 'but it's too damned dangerous.'

'I'll have to wash your mouth out with soap. Why is it dangerous, Sara? You're not talking about falling pregnant, I take it.'

'Do you want me to show you a prescription for the Pill?'

'That's not your problem.' His eyes looked very deeply into hers. 'You're in an agony of indecision. Give yourself to me and find yourself for ever trapped or renounce love altogether. That way you can go through life the fiery little radical. You'll have to bury the spectre of your father.'

'It's got nothing to do with my father. My father is a brilliant man.'

'And his effect on you has been catastrophic. You need a strong man, Sara, but the strong men are the ones you fight. It's easier to have a comfortable sit-in with Palmer, for example. By the way, he doesn't actually need you any more to complete the portrait.'

'You asked him?'

'I told him.'

'You had no right!'

'I can speak for the woman I want for my wife.'

'Oh no,' she said wildly. 'Not now. Not *ever*!'

He put his hand through her hair and tilted back her head. 'Can you really see me believing that?'

'Men on high horses have a long way to fall.'

'Even a spitting little cat responds if you feed it and pet it. I really feel I have to tame you.'

'*Guy?*' Despite herself her voice trembled.

'Hush! Lie still.'

'I can't.'

'No, you can't, you sensuous creature.' His hand smoothed her nape, her neck, her shoulder. 'Your hair's longer.' It fell well past her shoulders. 'I think I'll brush it one night. Hair like yours is rare. I'd like to see it reproduced in my daughter.'

'Stop that! It gives me the creeps.'

'You know I'll be very gentle with you.'

'I don't know that at all.' She closed her eyes and he raised her up closer to him.

'You know you've had this coming all night.'

When his mouth closed over hers she shivered in a painful ecstasy but she lacked the will to end it. She was a woman. She was vanquished. A victim. Only he wasn't hurting her at all. He was kissing her, caressing her in a way that brought the helpless tears to her eyes. It was mastery, certainly, but she was a very willing slave. What she was giving up was herself: her woman's body to a man's dominion. How could she fight it when it seemed formed for his hand?

When he released the zipper of her dress she had an idea to cry out, but before it was properly formed he had peeled the silk away from her breasts. She reached up and put her arms around his neck, and he drew in his breath sharply as though a whip had flicked his skin.

'Tell me you love me.' His voice was harsh with leashed passion.

'Oh, *Guy!*' She bit at his top lip with soft, savage desperation. 'The blood is pounding in my ears.'

'Maybe so.' His hands on her breasts had a stunning sensuality. 'But you can't bring yourself to say it.'

'Why on this particular night?' she moaned. Commitment was as terrible as truth.

He gave a harsh little bark of laughter and held her away by her hair. 'Just how long do you think I can keep this up, this role of *Cousin* Guy? It's the thinnest disguise there is. I want you, Sara. *Right now.* I want to make you cry out, I love you, I love you. Over and over. I want to hear your soft excited voice at the advance of a lover. I don't want to stop. I want to go on and on. I want you so much I've had to build up an iron control. Yet I have to admire yours. Every word that falls from your lips is denied in my arms.'

'I am as I am,' she very softly intoned, nudging away his restraining hand and kissing the bronze column of his throat. 'Your skin has the faintest hint of incense.'

'Maybe I've been burning it to a love-goddess.' His hand slid down her naked back. 'If I picked you up and carried you to my lair would you scream?'

'Yes.'

His jewelled eyes passed over her slender form. 'I'd very much like to see you without the rest of this dress.'

'I'm not such a brave woman.'

'You're exquisite enough. Are you asking me to hold off, Sara?' He brought his lips back to her throbbing mouth.

'Yes.' Without Clare in the house she would have been doomed.

'I can just manage that if you lock your door. It's apparent you're a model of virtue and I'd better respect it.'

'I don't know if I *could* say no if we were on our own,' she felt bound to admit.

'So you're not impregnable, little one?'

'No.' Her voice shook.

'Having Clare in the house is an influencing factor for me too, just in case you think my will-power is something special. Denying you is agony, Sara, but I'm determined not to force you into anything no matter how I feel. On the other hand, I'm not waiting for you to break me down any further.'

'What an idea!' she tried to joke.

'You've got one week,' he told her, a bright glitter in his eyes.

'One *week*?' She looked up at him.

'Come, come, Sara, you can't sleep on your own forever.'

'I read a lot.' She whispered.

'You won't be reading with me.' Those golden eyes were unwavering on her face.

'No.'

'Well, then...?'

I love you, she thought. I love you so much I would die if you ever stopped loving me. It was what she wanted to say, but the spoken admission was too awesome.

'Sara?' His voice was very deep and steady. 'You'll be safe with me. Very safe. You don't need all those defences.' He lowered his head and kissed her mouth.

'A week.'

He turned his head so that he could catch her whisper.

'A week, Guy. That's a promise.'

CHAPTER NINE

WAYNE unveiled Sara's finished portrait to an audience. As well as Val and Sara, Leigh unexpectedly arrived.

It was a large canvas, some four feet square, showing a three-quarter-length Sara seated sideways, her face towards the viewer against a background of lilac hills, evergreen tropical trees and a dense, jewel-blue sky. Sara was wearing one of the saris Clare had given her and the total effect was brilliant; a portrait that was both grand and intimate. Sara had been very carefully posed, her hands, so difficult to paint, arranged just so, but the painting was a marvel of spontaneity and great natural charm.

'I've never seen anything so beautiful, so elegant in my life!' Val went into raptures. 'You never catch my boy off balance. And what a model you make, Sara! Your hair, your skin, your eyes! One can get a marvellous *feel* of hair and silk and flesh. Wayne hasn't done anything like it.'

'You haven't even *begun* to see the limits of my talents!' Wayne announced modestly. 'Like it, Sara?'

'I'm speechless!' Good as she knew him to be, Sara had not been fully prepared for such a superb painting. 'You're quite right. You're capable of anything when you extend yourself.'

'That's true!' Val's large brown eyes were full of happy tears. 'He's never been described as a portrait painter, but this could easily win one of the big prizes. You can see that he loves you!'

'Oh, for God's sake!' Leigh suddenly shouted, nearly hysterically. 'He loves *me*.'

None of them had turned to see Leigh's reaction, now they found her thin, tanned face flushed with wild colour. 'Why don't you have the guts to tell them, Wayne?'

'I really don't see how he can!' Wayne's mother said in a shrill voice. 'You saw what happened when you were engaged? It wasn't a pleasant time then, and it hasn't been a pleasant time since.'

'What's happened, Wayne?' Sara asked.

'He's never *stopped* loving me!' Leigh wailed. 'The best thing he's ever done! He's painted *me*. My portrait could be just as famous. His only interest in Sara is her hair, her white skin. He thought it might be a challenge to paint.'

'You come over here this morning trying to upset us!' Val's small, pleasant face was a study in astonishment and resentment. 'I know what's changed *your* mind. You made a fool of yourself running after Guy Trenton and when you couldn't bring that off—I could have *told* you—you remembered my son. He's a success now, isn't he? His paintings are starting to fetch big money. I seem to recollect your dear father called him a bludger and similar other nasty words. Well, let him eat them.'

'I don't care *what* Daddy says!' Leigh made the extraordinary announcement. 'We've had a serious rift.'

'You are a dark horse, aren't you?' Sara said mildly. 'Was that what you wanted to tell Wayne about?'

'I have told him,' Leigh pointed out very irritably. 'At the party when you were carrying on with that television guy. You couldn't resist it, could you? I never drink myself.'

'Oddly enough, neither do I. The occasional glass of wine,' Sara said gently. 'I'm going to ignore your slanderous remarks because you're obviously upset, but if you decide to repeat them, I know all about the law.'

'Oh, absolutely, she does.' Wayne backed Sara up. 'Her father is a famous QC.'

'Yes, I am upset,' Leigh muttered by way of an apology. 'I know perfectly well he was chasing you.'

'What has all this got to do with anything?' Val asked briskly.

'Leigh wants us to start again,' Wayne told his mother reluctantly.

'Don't be silly, darling!' she returned forcibly. 'She let you down once, she'll do it again. She's cold and spoilt and malicious. She cares nothing for your work. You must know Sara is the girl for you.'

'No, Val.' Sara put her hand on the older woman's arm. 'I hope I can continue to number you and Wayne among my good friends, but Wayne and I are not in love with each other.'

'But he told me only the other day he was!' Val looked across at her son, perplexed. 'Were you lying to me, boy?'

'I *feel* for Sara, Mamma,' Wayne said. 'She's so warm inside and lovely to look at, but I've known from the beginning she wasn't for me. She's too good for me, can't you see that? Part of me willed things to happen but I always *knew*. Sara values qualities in a man I haven't got. Even if she did love me, I'd let her down dreadfully. No, Mamma, I have to face hard reality. I'm no great shakes and neither is Leigh. We can take one another as we are.'

'Well, *thanks*!' Leigh picked up a pottery plate and dashed it to the floor. 'I'm no great shakes, am I?'

'You'd better tidy that up!' Val looked in absolute shock from Leigh's face to the floor.

'Don't worry, Mum, I never liked it,' Wayne started to pick the pieces up and Leigh crouched down to help him, her fingers shaking so much Wayne twisted and kissed her on the cheek.

'You know what I mean, pet. We kind of focus on ourselves, don't we? Both of us have been spoilt rotten. Mamma has always doted on me, and your father has a lot to answer for. We need to work a bit on our characters.'

It was an emotional afternoon and Sara was glad to make an escape. Val and Wayne were wrestling aloud their anxieties at this proposed new way of life and the two girls left them to it.

'I'll drive you back into town, shall I?' Leigh asked hastily. 'I always knew there was going to be a "bloody day of reckoning".'

'You do *love* him, Leigh?' Sara asked as a wave of pity swept over her.

'Yes, yes,' Leigh answered shortly, backing away from the farmhouse as though all the devils in hell were after her. 'Of course I love him.'

'You've got a funny way of showing it.'

'So has he.'

'I can't argue with that one.' Sara gazed out at the cloud of dust Leigh was churning up, fascinated. 'Wayne is highly gifted, Leigh, but that alone doesn't ensure a great future. You can understand why Val is worried. She's put all her life into Wayne.'

'Hasn't she ever!' Leigh gritted.

'She's his *mother*! Wait till you're one yourself. What I'm trying to say is, are you going to help him, Leigh?'

'What business is it of yours?' Leigh's tanned cheeks flushed. 'You only dazzled Wayne for a time. It was a dream.'

'I like him. I like Val. I don't want to see either of them hurt. Nor you. Also, and I don't think I'm over-stating it, we need our artists. All of us. They enrich our existence. They show us the world through their very special eyes. Wayne is a fine artist, but he's going to need you to show a keen interest in his work.'

'I intend to find out more about it,' Leigh said with such finality that Sara had to believe her. 'Since I *am* my father's daughter, I should be able to run a business. I don't have a high appreciation level, like you, but I expect that to increase with the study I'm going to put in. Your portrait is beautiful. Absolutely beautiful. I've got eyes to see that.'

They parted almost amicably, and Sara wandered around the prosperous and picturesque township making a few purchases and filling in a little time before ringing for Tom to pick her up. With Wayne totally involved in calming his mother and staving off her near collapse there had been no question of his driving her back to the plantation. Leigh had not offered and Sara hadn't asked. Tom wouldn't mind coming for her.

Sara was making towards a phone booth to ring when a familiar brittle voice accosted her. 'Sara, what are *you* doing in town?'

One thing seemed to lead to another and Sara found herself a reluctant passenger in the Chadwick four-wheel drive.

'I'm really glad of this opportunity for the two of us to have a private chat,' Annabel told her, her pale eyes blazing. 'This little sojourn of yours is turning sour.'

'My dear, if it is I'd have to blame you!'

Annabel stiffened as though shot. 'You think of Guy as your hero, and he has taken you under his protection, but he's like that. Some men are natural protectors. It's been like that for thousands of years. Man the warrior, the great overlord who never failed to take care of the women and children. It's going on today. Take *me*. My relationship with Guy is highly complex and it goes back a long way. I'm crazy about him.'

'I'm sorry. It can't be particularly easy for you. Perhaps you should consider moving away.'

'Not *me*, you silly girl. *You!*' Annabel cried in furious astonishment. 'Some women are great over short distances, but I'm in for the marathon. This is my last race.'

'I wish you luck. You think Guy will marry you?'

'He's not marrying anyone else,' Annabel gritted.

'And how are you going to make him refuse other offers? It must be a terribly hard thing to face, and don't think I don't feel for you, but Guy doesn't love you.'

'*Doesn't* he?' Annabel coughed harshly. 'Let me present you with a few facts. We've been lovers for years. It was even going on when my husband was alive.'

'Gosh, he must have cried himself to sleep every night,' Sara remarked sympathetically, 'were it ever *true*!'

'You don't believe me?' Annabel turned off the town road. 'The young are very romantic. Guy has always turned to me for sexual gratification. I am, darling, what's known as good between the sheets.'

'I've a dark suspicion you're good at fantasising as well.'

'Don't you think he's been my lover?' Annabel asked angrily, furious at Sara's flippant tone.

'Maybe. At one time. He's not the parish priest. On the other hand I'm certain there was no involvement the time you were married. I know Guy. And I'm sure there's not now.'

'He'll come back to me,' Annabel cried in a quivering voice. 'He always does.'

'Then it's very odd indeed that he wants to marry *me*.'

Annabel was so violently shocked she almost lost control of the wheel. 'What?' Her voice cracked out like a whip.

'I'm sorry,' Sara said in a tone of one who really was. 'I know enough about loving to know about pain. Your feeling for Guy is like a prison without sun. You won't let yourself out.'

For answer Annabel got a steely grip on Sara's arm. 'Get out.'

'Gladly.' She resisted Annabel's shoving with all her might. 'Stop the car.'

'You can't be serious. Why don't you *jump*?'

'If *I* go, lady, you'll come with me!' Her fighting spirit overcame Sara's shock.

'Let *go*!' Annabel tried to slap her away.

'The hell I will!' Sara hung on. 'Do you want to kill us both?'

'Yes!' Annabel shouted, near hysterically.

'Sorry, I can't oblige.' Now Sara got her hand on the gear stick. The hand-brake was beyond her reach, but if she could just get the vehicle into reverse...

The Range Rover bucked like a wild outback brumby and Annabel, like the strange perverse creature she was, screamed a raging protest.

'What are you trying to do, wreck our bus?'

'I'd wreck a vehicle first before I'd let it wreck me. You're a nut, Annabel,' Sara cried disgustedly. 'I'm sure you've got a strait-jacket around some place.' She thrust open the door and jumped out.

'Oh, you bitch!' Annabel sobbed, trying unsuccessfully to put the vehicle into forward gear. 'Clive's not going to be at all pleased when he hears this.'

'Poor old Clive! You'd better run along now. It must be time for you to go back into your cage.'

'Just you wait!' Annabel roared.

It was too much for Sara; she laughed. Some days it was downright dangerous to get out of bed.

Annabel swung the Range Rover into a U-turn, and just in case she was harbouring any more murderous plans, Sara dashed behind a great mango tree laden with fruit. It was possible in the country silence to hear Annabel cursing violently. Sara watched, transfixed, as the vehicle tore off in the opposite direction. She cursed a little herself, but she couldn't match Annabel in any way. And why would she ever want to? Annabel was stark, raving *mad*. What else could one say about it?

The day, like all the days, was fine and brilliant. She would have a long walk. Her leg had grown a lot stronger with physiotherapy and exercise, but she wasn't looking forward to the trek before her. Perhaps she could cut across a field and go to look for a farmhouse. At moments like this one she realised how isolated the plantation was. She had no head cover of any kind and she had to protect herself from the tropical sun. The frond of one of the giant ferns was the best she could do.

She had been crunching along her way for the best part of thirty minutes when the sound of an approaching car engine made her turn her head. Astonishment. Relief. It was the Mercedes. She fixed her eyes on its shimmering bulk and as it came within one hundred yards of her, she forced herself into the middle of the road and waved her arms. She was breathless from the heat, her cotton voile shirt and soft slacks damp with sweat. Her long hair was soaked at the temples and nape and the humidity had given her creamy skin a hectic flush.

'For the love of God, Sara, what are you doing out here in the open?' Guy demanded violently, catching hold of her shoulder as she appeared to stagger.

'Oh, let me sit down,' she moaned. 'Is it *hot*! I think I've baked my brain.'

His brilliant eyes reflected a hard perplexity. He led her back to the car and put her into the passenger seat. 'No one but an idiot takes a long walk in the heat of the afternoon.' He put an examining hand on top of her billowing masses of red-gold curls. 'How did this happen?'

'How does anything happen up here?' she gasped, resting her hot head against the soft velour. 'I should have known Paradise was too much of a good thing.'

'You're dehydrated!' He swore violently, swinging back into the car and driving off at top speed. Seven minutes later they were bumping up a dirt track to a deserted farmhouse. A *For Sale* notice was nailed to the white picket fence but it was almost obscured by foaming masses of orange and gold lantana.

'Come inside.' He got an arm behind her and walked her up the rickety steps. The front door wasn't even locked and they made their way through the shadowy, silent bungalow to the kitchen at the rear of the house.

The water ran rusty at first, then crystal clear.

'Heaven, that's *heaven*!' Sara exulted as he splashed her face and neck with water. 'I might even take a shower.'

'Have a drink of water,' he advised her, cupping his hands. 'Don't gulp it. How are you feeling?'

'A little desperate until you came along. It's no fun walking along a long empty road with an immensity of blue sky and a blazing hot sun. It was fortunate I had the palm leaf for protection.'

He held her head back so that he could look down into her sun-flushed face. The glare alone was sufficient to burn.

'I don't know that there would be anything wrong with a shower,' he reasoned.

'It might bring me to life.'

He stayed outside the bathroom door as she stood rapturously under the cold cascades of water. It was difficult for anyone to appreciate just how marvellous a cold shower was until they had experienced being burned by a tropical sun.

'What are you doing in there?' he called, after a little while.

'Drowning.'

'I've found you something to dry yourself with.'

'I hope it's not a blanket.' She turned off the tap and pressed the water from her long hair.

'It's a tablecloth. It's big, long and perfectly clean. In fact it's scented with boronia.'

'Thank you.' She hopped out of the shower recess and waggled a hand outside the slightly ajar door.

A big spotted mirror showed her slender frame draped in yellow and white checked gingham, her long hair sliding down her back like a gleaming dark-red ribbon. She looked perfectly respectable, draped in a makeshift sarong. She might as well leave it on as drag on her damp bundle of clothes. Her shirt had sopped up most of the moisture.

'That must have cooled you off.' He flung her a shimmering gold glance then turned away decisively.

'I feel like a garden after rain.'

'I've never seen a woman who looked more like a flower. Let's get going.'

She padded after him, upset now that she was obviously taking up too much of his time. He had been heading towards town, probably on business. There was nothing else to do but obey his terse order.

He waited for her to precede him out of the front door but as she went to step out on to the bougainvillaea-wreathed veranda, she shrieked.

'Sara, stop it!' He pulled her back violently into his arms.

'Do you expect me to walk over the top of a snake?' Her heart was beating like a wild thing. 'It's there on the top stair.'

'Oh, *hell*!' he groaned, turning his dark head with what seemed a great effort. 'Look it's gone.'

Being so close to him turned her limbs to water. 'Hold me,' she shocked herself by pleading. 'If you loved me what could be more important than holding me?'

His arms tightened ominously. 'I'm trying to honour you, you little fool!'

'*Honour?*' She stared up in wonder at his taut, vital face.

'What kind of a seductress *are* you?' he asked with black humour. 'You don't seem to know what you do to me.'

'Do I drive you wild?' The desire she saw in his glittery eyes shook her to the core.

'If you don't, why are you blinking?'

'I just want you to hold me,' she whispered as though she were still out of breath.

'Don't ask me to spell it out, Sara,' he warned her harshly. 'I love you. I *want* you. That's why I'm trying to get out of here before it all turns to ravishment.'

A confusion of emotions played across her transparent face. What was love? Love was trust. Love was caring for the beloved more than one cared for oneself.

Her adolescent obsession with male oppression burned itself out in that instant. She was precious. Of great value.

'*Please,* darling.' He drew her for a moment against his breast.

Tenderness transfigured passion. Her beautiful eyes were enormous, darkly green. 'I love you,' she said for the very first time.

'Do you?' He seemed to be trying to look into her very heart.

'How could you not know?'

She heard his violent intake of breath, then as he stared down at her, she opened up her soft mouth, inviting, *pleading* with him to claim it.

'Too late,' he said. 'Too late.'

He propelled her back through the door, bringing his mouth down on hers with so much fire and passion she felt as if she were floating.

The very air was aflame.

'My love!'

Did she say it or did he?

Streamers of golden light came through the shutters and outside in the tulip tree a resident bird began to carol a piercingly sweet song.

She had no idea how they got there but they were on the long padded seat in the bay window. He was holding her as she half lay across him. His hands were moving over her with a clamorous swift urgency as the length of cotton began to unravel at her breasts.

'You are so *beautiful*!' He held her up and slightly away from him, an extreme hunger in his face. The soft material slid to her narrow waist where it held.

Her breasts were as high and perfect as any porcelain figurine and his hands cupped them exultantly while his mouth enclosed her open lips.

The rapture was unbearable. Tears streaked down her cheeks.

'I want you,' she begged. 'I was terrified, but I'm not now.'

'Sara!' It was a broken little groan.

The fierce flutterings in her body mounted. She was panting and palpitating like a bird. There was a great ambivalence in a woman's nature that drove a man to possess her even while she feared his domination.

'Yes, yes, *please*, Guy.'

He spun her so that she was beneath him, calling on his strong will. He was trying not to take advantage of her, of the unexpectedness of the situation, but she was tempting him terribly, inciting him to a soft violence.

The white and yellow cotton was the most fragile defence. His hand swept her, tracing, lingering, learning, while she lay there not thinking as the tide of sensation carried her further and further on. He could do whatever he wanted...whatever he wanted...her body was the most sensitive instrument and he alone would know its response.

'Sara!' He tasted her mouth, her throat, her breasts, the slight indentation on the flat, smooth curve of her stomach. 'I've *got* to stop.' It was a tormented rasp.

'No, no, I can't bear it. I love you. I trust you with my life.'

'Then I want everything to be perfect for you.' He held her by the shoulders. 'I want to coax you, caress you all through the night. I want to explore every secret place of your body. I want the right place and the right time. I want you to be my *wife*.'

She knew he meant every word he said. She flung her arm up and he kissed it.

The realisation came that the checked fabric had fallen in soft folds to the floor. She lay naked before his eyes, still spinning with desire. The quiet room was suffused with it, an atmosphere so tangible it had a velvety weight of its own.

His hand tightened over the long, delicate bones of her hip, his long, darkly tanned fingers kneading into the white satin flesh of her body. He did not take his hand away; neither did he move it down further, the authority of his mind controlling a fierce, hard-driving passion.

'Talk to me, Sara.'

'I want you,' she whispered rebelliously, the pupils of her eyes enlarged by tears. His hand slipped inches and she arched convulsively. 'I'm in your hands, Guy. Me. My life. My happiness. Everything. What you want you can have. Don't you see?'

'One of us has to decide for both of us. Are you going to fight it because it's me? What I want I want for *you*. Does that make any sense?'

Of course it did. She reached down and retrieved the gingham cloth. 'Who took this from me, you?'

His eyes were so brilliant they burned. 'Seeing you naked I could scarcely have you any other way.'

Yet he helped her drape it around herself as if she were a little girl.

'I never did find out what you were doing on the open road.'

'Nothing important.' She stood on tip-toe to press a deeply tender kiss to his throat, then his cleft chin. 'A little problem that's all been sorted out.'

'Don't give me that one, green eyes.' He reached for her and tucked her under his arm. 'You can tell me all about it in the car. *Your* life is *my* life, and it's only just begun.'

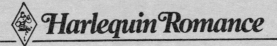# Harlequin Romance

Coming Next Month

Available in February wherever paperback books are sold, or through Harlequin Reader Service:

In the U.S.
901 Fuhrmann Blvd.
P.O. Box 1397
Buffalo, N.Y. 14240-1397

In Canada
P.O. Box 603
Fort Erie, Ontario
L2A 5X3

Keepsake

Harlequin Books

You're never too young to enjoy romance. Harlequin . . . and Keepsake, young-adult romances destined to win hearts, for your daughter.

Pick one up today and start your daughter on her journey into the wonderful world of romance.

Two new titles to choose from each month.